MACHOPONI
A Prance With Death

Written by
Lotus Rose
Illustrated by Emma Björk

SPUNK GOBLIN PRESS

SPUNK GOBLIN PRESS
AN IMPRINT OF ERASERHEAD PRESS

ERASERHEAD PRESS
205 NE BRYANT
PORTLAND, OR 97211

WWW.ERASERHEADPRESS.COM

ISBN: 1-933929-79-0

Machoponi *and the* Lost Blue Ball

7

Name: Machoponi
Type: Bedroom Eyes Miniponi
Body: Purple
Hair: Violet
Eyes: Green
Quote: "It's so hard being macho!"

Machoponi gazed into the landscape of the Dark Kingdom, with a scowl on his face. He was waiting for some of the undead soldiers to come out from the large, olive green military tent about thirty-five feet away. The soldiers would probably be waking up soon, because it was almost dusk.

It never ceased to amaze him how the whole world changed within such a short distance. On the side where Machoponi stood was the Pastel Kingdom, with its green grass, blue skies and butterflies...but then all the bright colors abruptly stopped and on the other

Lotus Rose

8

side of a crack in the earth, the sky was gray and dark, and the grass was brown.

That crack in the earth was the ancient Jagged Line from the Great Dividing and was just a leaping distance away from Machoponi. The Jagged Line stretched all the way across Poniworld and split it in half. It was the line that was deadly to cross. During the Great Dividing, the earth had quaked and a crack formed in the ground. On that fateful day, all the ponies on the other side of the Jagged Line had been transformed from pastel ponies into undead ponies.

Machoponi felt his heartbeat quicken—over there in the Dark Kingdom, some of the members of the undead army were coming out of the tent.

With mean eyes, six of them came out the front opening, and looked around suspiciously. Their coats were dark gray, their tails and manes were scraggly and dirty silver, as was typical of the undead. One of them had a mohawk hairstyle.

Their black eyes narrowed upon seeing Macho. Macho had been there to greet them at the same time for the past three days.

"Hey sissy!" one of them yelled. That one nudged two others, then the whole group turned and mooned Machoponi.

Machoponi gave them the tongue back.

"Bet you wish you had some chocolate mints!"

one of the soldiers taunted.

"Chocolate mints are for losers!" Machoponi called back.

Their hateful scowls faltered slightly as they saw what Macho held under his front right hoof: it was a blue ball. Jealousy showed on their undead faces as they gazed at the ball. It was the first time they'd seen it. Machoponi had been practicing with it for weeks. Now was his chance to show off.

He flipped the ball up and bounced it repeatedly on his knee.

The dead-in-the-eyes stares from across the Jagged Line chilled Machoponi straight to the bone. He trembled slightly, but he was absolutely determined not to fumble in front of them, and he quickly regained his confident command of the ball.

As they realized that they couldn't intimidate him into flubbing, one by one, members of the group left to use the latrines. That was why they had exited the tent in the first place—Machoponi knew their habits.

The undead ponies were ignoring him now, or at least trying to pretend they were, but Machoponi could see their every-once-in-a-while sideways glances to where he was, and the brief flashes of jealousy.

Normally, the citizens of each kingdom kept on their side of the cracked earth, because if a living pony entered the Dark Kingdom, it would slowly make

them sicker and eventually kill them, and if an undead pony crossed over into the Pastel Kingdom, it would immediately cause them to disintegrate.

10

Machoponi bounced the ball higher up off of his knee, then bounced it twice on the top of his head, then went back to bouncing it on his knee.

The undead ponies across the line tried hard to look unimpressed. Most of the ponies had used the latrines already and had returned to the group.

Macho let the ball come to rest on top of his knee, then tipped his leg so the ball rolled down the front of his right leg, then held it balanced on his hoof, then kicked and rolled the ball back up his leg, rolled it over the back of his neck and down his front left leg, then held it balanced on his front left hoof.

The undead ponies who were watching him scoffed and rolled their eyes.

Machoponi grinned and wriggled his nose mockingly. He kicked the ball high up into the air. When the ball came back down, he bounced it off his tail, sending the ball into a forward arc—he stood, staring at the undead ponies with an innocent expression as the ball hung in the air—it landed eight feet in front of him on the ground inside the Dark Kingdom! He'd given it just the right amount of back spin so that it didn't bounce, but hugged the ground and rolled backwards...he lifted his front right leg, where it rolled

neatly underneath his hoof and he stepped on it and held it there.

The undead stood with their jaws dropped.

Machoponi grinned a little. They had been quite unsuccessful in ignoring him.

The leading officer, indicated by his dirty-silver mohawk, who Machoponi knew was named Dolph, swore angrily, then bid his group to follow him and they all went back inside the tent.

Machoponi laughed hysterically.

It felt so good to be macho.

11

He was laughing so hard, he had to bend his head down. But then his leg twitched and he accidentally nudged the ball, and it started rolling quickly toward the Jagged Line!

He stopped laughing.

His eyes went wide.

All he could do was watch as the ball sped across the line, into the dark side, and it just kept rolling, until it finally came to rest a few feet in front of the tent.

Macho muttered something rude under his breath.

He pouted severely. He had no choice but to go retrieve it.

This ball was special because it had a spell put on it that made it unpopable. A magician had cast the spell to honor Macho's war hero grandfather, Studponi. The

ball, which had been a gift from Studponi's daughter, had been the only thing motivating Studponi to stay alive as he lay hiding in a trench surrounded by Nazi ponies. Studponi survived his ordeal and passed the ball down to Macho's father, who had just given it to Macho on his 16th birthday. And now Machoponi had lost it in a matter of a few weeks.

He pouted severely again.

12

Well, he had no choice but to cross over into the dark side and retrieve it. He knew that being there would make him sick—those foolish ponies who went into the Dark Kingdom on a dare, even for a brief moment, would be ill for several days. He was lucky, at least, that all the soldiers were inside the tent and didn't see him lose his ball. He supposed that most other ponies his age might be too afraid to cross the Jagged Line, at least not without other ponies to help. But he wasn't a regular pony. He was Machoponi and he had a reputation to protect.

He took a determined breath, muttered to himself, "It's so hard being macho," then began walking to get his ball back!

He stood right on the edge. He'd never crossed the Jagged Line before. His legs began to tremble.

He looked to the tent. The past three days, when the undead ponies had gone into the large military tent, they'd stayed inside for hours. That was when

Machoponi

Machoponi would leave, because there was no point in waiting around.

If he was quiet enough, he was sure he could get his ball back without incident. As long as he didn't stay over there too long, there would be no risk of becoming undead.

He closed his eyes and took the plunge.

A chill immediately engulfed his body.

He shuddered, opened his eyes and everything looked murkier. It was startling to see and feel how different it was from the Pastel Kingdom.

As if to reassure himself that his homeland was still there, he jerked his head to look behind him. The sudden movement made his stomach lurch, but the sight of his home comforted him.

He was feeling nauseous and weak. The air had a sickly-sweet smell like rotting garbage.

It was just like ponies said it was.

Machoponi wasn't looking forward to being sick the next few days, but he knew he was a lot tougher than most other ponies, because he was Machoponi, and he knew he could stay inside the Dark Kingdom longer than most, at least long enough to get his ball back.

With wobbly knees, trying to be as quiet as possible, he walked to the ball. Quickly, he nudged it toward the Jagged Line. It rolled on the ground, then

13

14

went across, coming to a rest a few feet past it.

He sighed with relief.

The ball was safe now. The undead couldn't cross the Jagged Line: it was said to literally cause their flesh to melt.

But now his curiosity was piqued by something else. He cocked his head to listen. He could hear strange noises coming from the inside of the tent. A couple of the soldiers were cackling maniacally. One of them kept saying, "Mmmm."

Macho wondered what the hell was going on in there.

Then, even though he knew it might not be such a smart idea, but because he was so overwhelmingly macho, he slipped his head inside the front flap of the tent and yelled, "You're all a bunch of morons!"

The next part of his plan was to take off galloping until he was safely on the other side of the Jagged Line. But instead of running, Machoponi's jaw dropped as he gazed in wide wonder at the scene before his eyes.

They were gambling! They were all standing around a green baccarat table, which Macho knew was used for playing a card game. Next to their cards were piles of fruit, which they seemed to be betting with! It was scandalous! Gambling was absolutely forbidden on the pastel side, but apparently there was no decency here. How could they allow it without all the ponies falling

into depravity? But what was even worse was that there was a marble table off to the side piled with chocolate candy! Machoponi guessed that they were chocolate mints. He'd never personally seen any, but he knew ponies who said they had. Chocolate mints had been forbidden on the pastel side, and all the recipes were said to be destroyed—over time, the pastel ponies had forgotten how to make them. But the undead ponies in the Dark Kingdom made and consumed them all the time—and they were known to sometimes smuggle them across the Jagged Line in trade. Ponies were said to get some kind of "good feeling" from the mints.

15

But the elders said that it caused you to lose discipline and eventually ruined your body and caused you to die. But the undead were already dead, so maybe it didn't matter to them. Besides, the elders seemed to lie about a lot of things.

The six ponies in the tent stared dumbly back at Machoponi.

Then they all busted out laughing!

The leading officer of the group, Dolph, grinned widely—he had mesmerizing dimples and the sharp incisors of the undead. He replied, "It seems that *you're* the moron. Don't you know that crossing the Jagged Line will kill you?"

Macho gritted his teeth. He knew that Dolph was telling the truth.

Lotus Rose

So if he wasn't stupid, he would leave now, while he still had a chance, but that macho part of his soul kept pushing him to do aggressive things.

Maybe he could just administer a quick bludgeoning...he didn't know how he could live with himself if he turned tail and galloped away.

16

Macho growled to himself during his moment of indecision, his mind switching back and forth between the two choices. Then in the interest of self-preservation, he took off galloping. But then he stopped halfway to the Jagged Line.

Something was itching at the back of his mind.

He looked back toward the tent. One of the soldiers was just now sticking his head out of the front, with a goofy grin on his face.

Macho felt a strange twinge of envy. He wished that he could be happy like that, rather than tormented and edgy. What was making the undead ponies so gleeful? Was it the thrill of gambling? The chocolate mints? He put on his best endearing grin, then started walking back toward the tent. "Hey!" he called out. "Can I try some of those chocolate mints?"

Now all the undead ponies had stepped outside. They eyed Machoponi suspiciously, then looked to see what Dolph decided. Dolph nodded—his mohawk wobbled slightly, then he called out, "Our chocolate mints are the greatest! If you become one of us undead,

you can have them everyday! Why don't you come inside and try some?"

"Really?" Macho called back. "You won't try to kill me?"

"Of course not," Dolph replied, "if you don't try to kill *us*." The other undead ponies chuckled. "But listen, we'll let you go, and you can tell everypони about the chocolate mints so they can cross over and become converted. It'll work out for both of us." He grinned.

17

Machoponi had a habit of acting without thinking a lot of the time. All he knew at that moment, was that he really wanted to see what all the fuss was about with the chocolate mints. He decided he would trick the undead ponies into letting their guards down, which would make it easier for him to escape later. So he started walking back toward the group of undead ponies and said, "Really, I've been thinking a lot lately about maybe joining you undead. You seem to have a lot of fun. It gets pretty boring with everything being pastel all the time."

The undead ponies stepped inside the tent and he followed them. They all eagerly walked to the table piled with chocolate mint candies, then started nudging with their noses and taking pieces into their mouths. There was a strange scent in the air, which Machoponi assumed was mint. He bit his lip as he watched them with excitement rising up inside him.

18

Dolph fixed Macho with a big grin, with his dimples deep and prominent. He nudged a chocolate in Macho's direction on the table. "Go ahead and give it a go," Dolph said coaxingly.

Macho was feeling afraid, even though he was usually overly brave. The candy looked brown and kind of gross, actually. He remembered the stories he'd heard and asked, "Is it green on the inside?"

"Yeah," Dolph replied, "that's the mint part. It mixes with the chocolate inside your mouth and wooooo." He blew out a shuddering breath into the air in front of him.

Machoponi arched his brow. "It's that good, huh?"

"There's nothing better."

There was a part inside of Machoponi, a dark side, that had always remained hidden. It was the part moving his legs forward, causing his head to dip. He'd just have a little. What could a little hurt?

He took the candy into his mouth. He bit in—the taste was foreign to him. He began to chew, then the cooling sensation hit him, mixing in with the dark chocolate beginning to melt in his mouth.

It was like a shooting cold chill going throughout his mouth and his head. It felt so good. It was a lot like the chill he had felt upon entering the dark side, but this chill wasn't bad at all, and now he realized how

Machoponi

a chill could actually feel very good. It was a feeling of glorious ecstasy. He closed his eyes and his eyelids began to twitter. He opened his mouth and blew out a breath of cool air. Now he knew what all the fuss was about.

He opened his eyes to see everyponi staring at him.

Dolph's dimpled grin slowly crept up the side of his face. "It's good, huh?"

Macho just stood looking at him, trying to savor every moment of that minty chocolate flavor in his mouth.

Dolph fixed him with a flirtatious stare. "It's all yours, if you join us. We can make your death pleasant."

Macho tried to remain outwardly calm, despite the rising fear inside of him, which came partly from the fact that the undead ponies were blocking the only way out of the tent, and partly from the fact that he was actually considering joining.

"Have another piece," Dolph was saying now, with that pointy grin of his, and now all the ponies were approaching Macho. When they got close enough,

Machoponi had no doubt that they would pounce. He scanned his eyes madly around the inside of the tent, looking for a way out.

But then he attained a sudden, brilliant surge of thought—the influence of the mints had cleared the obscuring clutter in his mind.

20

In a sudden mental jump, he imagined himself in the future, obsessed with attaining the next chocolate. Just like everything else in life, he knew that it would become "not enough" and he would constantly be seeking to increase the fix. So he knew that the way to get the soldiers' attention off of him was to offer *them* a better fix.

The chocolate mints caused his mind to form connections it normally wouldn't. He could see now in his mind's eye, a glorious combination:

strawberry and banana

The undead ponies were taken aback by the expression of self-satisfaction upon Macho's face.

"What?" muttered Dolph, taking a step backward.

Machoponi nodded his head over to the baccarat table piled with fruit. He spoke slowly, with blank eyes, like a poni possessed: "Take the strawberry and banana, mush them together. Eat them, then follow with a chocolate mint."

Machoponi

Expressions of fear came across the undead ponies' faces.

Dolph chuckled uneasily. "That's ridiculous," he said. "Strawberry and banana are two separate fruits. It is unnatural to combine them!"

"What, are you scared? Of course it's unnatural! That's why it's so good! Do it," Macho stated simply. "It'll be an amazing rush."

The group of undead ponies nodded eagerly. That was all they needed to hear.

"Here," Macho lulled sweetly, as he walked to the baccarat table, "I'll show you." He nudged three strawberries next to a banana. He began to peel the banana with his teeth as the undead ponies watched. His distraction was working. They were completely enthralled.

He took a bite of banana, then took a strawberry into his mouth. He swallowed and his head lurched back—he bumped into a poni behind him and started shuddering.

"Quick, give me a chocolate mint!" Macho shouted. One of the undead guided him to the chocolate mint table, because Macho's legs were shaking so much that he could barely walk. His eyes were rolling up into the back of his head and his mouth was writhing. He was whimpering, and he dropped the chocolate mint twice before getting it into his mouth.

21

And then he was holding that delectable candy in his mouth—he was biting down and it was mixing and melting in his mouth!

Macho looked around at the hooves of the other ponies and he realized that he had fallen down. He raised his gaze to look at them. He had to close one eye, because it was difficult to look out of both at the same time.

The soldiers were gathered around the baccarat table, with strawberries and bananas in front of them. Their eyes were rolling in their heads—they looked insane.

They were completely ignoring Machoponi, so he simply stood up and walked out of the tent. He then began to gallop toward the Jagged Line. But he was having trouble galloping straight—the Jagged Line seemed to be shifting to his right, and then he heard a call behind him: "Hey, get him! He's getting away!"

He looked behind him to see the group of soldiers spreading out from the tent, like a blooming flower of doom, veering off in various crooked lines. Dolph was the only one who seemed to be able to run somewhat straight, and he was quickly catching up.

"I'm gonna kill you!" Dolph yelled.

Briefly, their gazes locked, and what Machoponi saw in those eyes terrified him. He tried to calm himself and focus on reaching the Jagged Line. If he could just get across, he would be okay.

Machoponi

Macho turned his head forward. He was getting closer to the Jagged Line, but he could hear the sounds of Dolph's hooves closing in on him.

Machoponi crossed the Jagged Line and the world seemed to explode with pastel colors.

He gave a sigh of relief then stopped and turned around in order to mock Dolph. But his eyes widened as he saw Dolph still galloping toward him! Dolph's face was contorted with a grimace so hate-filled that it almost looked like he was smiling.

23

Dolph came closer and closer as Machoponi watched, frozen in fear. Machoponi tried to turn around and start running again, but his body was too slow to respond.

Dolph was almost upon him. Machoponi shouted out, "The line!" in a desperate attempt to make Dolph stop.

Dolph galloped to within five feet from Machoponi, but then an expression of fear came across his face, and he tried to come to a complete halt all of a sudden while he was directly over the Jagged Line, with his front half in the Pastel Kingdom and his back half in the Dark Kingdom. Dolph howled in pain as he dug his back legs into the ground.

The wrenching movement tore his body in half. Momentum caused his two front legs to keep stumbling forward as his back legs catapulted themselves back and

fell over, spraying a cloud of blood into the air and trailing intestines onto the ground.

24

Machoponi stepped to the side as Dolph's front half sprinted past him, then crashed face down next to the blue ball...then his tummy and intestines plopped over so that he was laying on his side. Dolph wriggled on the ground for a few seconds with terrified eyes while cursing and spitting up blood, then his body went still.

Macho cautiously approached Dolph's front half and tapped it with his hoof. The flesh felt soggy—it was already starting to disintegrate.

He looked back into the Dark Kingdom to see Dolph's back half twitching in a pool of blood.

The undead ponies seemed to be dazed by what happened. After several moments, one of them slurred, "More strawrana," then they all turned around and headed back to the tent.

Machoponi nudged the blue ball with his hoof—it had a few spatters of blood on it. Solemnly, he headed back to his village. He felt quite ill and knew he would be sick for the next few days. He squinted his eyes, because the Pastel Kingdom seemed so bright after having been in the Dark Kingdom.

Machoponi

The Legend of Machoponi
Part the First

25

O, hear the tale of Machoponi,
Who longed to call fair Dust his "lovely."
But she would never look his way,
And by his side, she would not stay.

A Hero with blue ball was he,
'Cross Jagged Line he pranced bravely,
With tender scowl and broken heart,
The torn two halves so far apart.

Like licking ice cream gives such pain,
With throbbing hurting of the brain.
So, pain can come upon Fate's breeze,
To punish Lust, just like brain freeze.

And Beauty draws his lovesick gaze.
He stares at Dust with heart ablaze!
Like sprinkles atop ice cream surprise,
Bring cold that causes your demise,
Dust gets in your eyes.

Crossing the Line

26

"You think you're sooooo tough," Clint mockingly called out. Machoponi narrowed his eyes and tried to keep the tears from welling up. He blinked them away. Behind Clint, five of the popular guyponies grinned viciously.

Why did trouble always seem to find him, even though he was never looking for it? Machoponi threw a scowl at Clint, the jerk of the village.

Then Machoponi sighed, because he just couldn't believe it! Dust, his #1 crush, walked out from behind the group then stood at Clint's side! She stared back at Macho with her big, ruby-red eyes, drawing his eyes into hers. He had always thought she was the cutest poni in the entire village, with the most beautiful color scheme of burgundy tail and mane on a white body. Machoponi didn't know why she hung around so much with Clint and his crew—Clint was a total jerk, and his blue body and green hair wasn't very attractive. Right now, Dust's burgundy mane rippled and whipped in

the wind and lapped at the soft curve of her flank and the vertical red jagged scar there. The pendant that she always wore around her neck twisted and untwisted. It was a ruby in the shape of half a heart—a jagged line was on its right side, as if the other half of the heart had been torn away.

Clint continued his verbal barrage. "You're not the only one who can cross the line. You really aren't anything but a big sissy, and I'm gonna prove it!"

Machoponi glanced at Clint's hooves; they were a few inches away from the crack in the earth known as the Jagged Line. On the other side of that line was the Dark Kingdom, a grim land where the undead ponies roamed. About three months ago, Machoponi had been there. He shuddered as he remembered. He had been sick for three days after that, and he feared his soul still hadn't recovered.

27

Macho lifted his chin and stared into Clint's eyes, then said, "I *really* wouldn't do that if I were you, Clint. What are you trying to prove?"

Clint scowled, then replied, "That you aren't as great—as *macho* as you think you are. I'm tired of you acting like you're the only one tough enough to cross the line."

Macho pouted as he felt the gaze of the eyes of all those ponies—and especially that special pair of eyes—those of Dust.

Macho looked down at his blue ball then at the ground around them. It was almost twilight and their bodies cast long shadows—the shadows looked almost as if they were trying to run away from the Jagged Line.

His own arrogance was coming back to haunt him, because even though Machoponi had been sick for days, he had faked that he was fine, all to appear tough in the eyes of all the other ponies.

The whole village had lavished Machoponi with praise and adoration, which of course, made Clint fume with jealousy, because Clint wanted to be the alpha male of the village. Ever since they were young colts, they had been in fierce competition.

Clint lifted his front right hoof....

"Don't...." Machoponi pleaded, trying to let his voice reveal the genuine concern that he felt.

"Why? Because you don't want everyone to know what a sissy you are?"

Machoponi made the decision right then to sacrifice his own pride to save Clint. "Clint," Macho said while trying to appear humble, "I felt horrible for a week after I crossed the line. I wouldn't recommend it—not at all."

"Cuz you're a sissy?"

"No...because it hurt. A lot."

Clint faltered just a little, so Machoponi knew there was some hope that he might back out of it.

Machoponi

Machoponi just needed to give Clint a way to save face. But instead of backing away, Clint looked around at the faces of all his buddies. Unfortunately, Clint had a reputation to uphold just like Machoponi did. They were two peas in a pod, and controlled by the same social forces.

"It's stupid, Clint," Macho scolded, "and besides..." he gestured with his chin to the olive green military tent on the dark side about fifteen feet away, "how do you know that Darkeyes and his platoon aren't going to come out?"

Clint's face registered absolutely no fear at all, which surprised Macho.

Darkeyes was the leading officer of the platoon of undead ponies inside the military tent. The undead ponies usually stayed inside during the day, but as Machoponi himself had experienced, sometimes they didn't do as they were expected.

Clint grinned smugly, and Dust's eyes gazed admiringly at Clint as he said, "Darkeyes is a sissy like you. If he gets within five feet of me, I'll kick his ass. I might even push him across the line! It'll be like a little trophy!"

Macho glanced at Dust to gauge her reaction to Clint's words. It seemed to Machoponi that Dust shuddered and grinned a little—was it from excitement or fear or nervousness? Perhaps she was grinning

29

because she thought Clint was a fool. Because that's what he was.

Because when living ponies cross the line into the Dark Kingdom, it is fatal to them within fifteen minutes. The undead ponies can't cross the Jagged Line at all, because it is immediately fatal to them.

But a few foolish male ponies would purposefully cross the line to show how tough they were. A few ponies, like Darkeyes, had even lost their lives that way. Of course, they were immediately reanimated as a new member of the undead, but they could never return home again, and they were shunned by the ponies of the Pastel Kingdom. Many of those lost ponies would stand for hours on the edge of the line, with mournful expressions, trying to keep contact with their friends and family who avoided them. But within a day or two, the Dark Kingdom transformed their appearance and personality—and they became typical undead jerks.

It was said that when Darkeyes had crossed the line, he had been trying to impress Dust as well. Machoponi glanced at her face, trying to read her expression. She was so beautiful.

And now he had to admit to himself that part of the reason he didn't want Clint to cross was because of the sense of rivalry. Macho remembered how Dust had looked at him after he himself had crossed the line. There had been a glow of admiration in her eyes all that

week, and there had even been a few instances of her looking down shyly.

He remembered the look in Dust's eyes as she had gazed at him, trembling slightly, her breathing deep and out of control. She had grown afraid, she told him, and she liked that feeling.

It had become clear over the years that Dust was one of those girls who liked "danger."

That look in her eyes had been what he'd wanted to see all his life, but what he'd only seen in his dreams or fantasies. For one week, that look had been directed at him—but then it had disappeared from her face when he didn't do anything else exciting. She was thrilled by the other guy ponies who'd mock-fight to impress her, and she flirted with the local sports stars. But Macho didn't do sports or unnecessary fights, so when Dust looked at him, she had the blank expression and glazed eyes of boredom.

31

Clint's hoof was hovering, inching closer to the Jagged Line. Dust watched in anticipation and Machoponi held his breath, and the gang of goofballs watched, waiting for the show.

"Please!" Macho shouted desperately. He thought for a moment, then said, "I don't think Dust really wants to watch you do something stupid. It would upset her." All heads turned toward Dust, and all eyes locked upon her face, trying to read her expression. A tender blush—

in a shade paler than her burgundy mane—crept up the sides of her neck and bloomed on her face.

She bowed her head down and smiled a trembling, nervous grin—at least that's what it looked like to Machoponi. *Surely* she couldn't be amused by all of this!

32

Clint's words almost tripped over each other as he proclaimed, "I tell you what. If Dust wishes it, I will not cross."

And then what followed was a long pause. Dust just kept looking down, her chest shuddering.

Clint huffed, then set one hoof on the ground in the dark side.

Clint glanced at Dust to read her expression.

Dust looked back at him, winked, then grinned.

Clint's male groupies whooped their encouragement.

Then Clint scowled at Macho while talking out the side of his mouth to his clique: "Perhaps I should *dance* across!" he proclaimed as they chuckled. Then he made a little hop-scooch movement, setting all four of his hooves on the ground inside the Dark Kingdom.

Clint's remark was a dig at Machoponi, because Macho had recently discovered a love of dance. He had been practicing in private, using ancient texts. Somehow Clint had found out and had challenged him to a dance off at the Promenade the following week.

Machoponi

Clint took a few steps into the dark side then turned to face them all. He looked around him in mock shock, then yelled to Macho, "Is *this* supposed to be it? Is *this* supposed to be what made you so sick? What a sissy! I hardly feel a thing!"

All the other guy ponies snickered and shot Macho hateful looks.

And now Macho, even though he didn't want to, was letting his pride take over his behavior as he said, "Clint! I stayed past the line much longer than you! You haven't even been there a minute! I stayed at *least* an hour!" He was exaggerating, of course.

33

Clint backed up further into the Dark Kingdom to illustrate his toughness. A strained grin crept up the side of his face.

Clint began mocking Macho by doing very clumsy ballet steps. "Look, I'm *Sissy*-poni!" Clint proclaimed as he leapt to his left and almost stumbled. Everyone laughed, except Machoponi, who pouted severely.

Macho snarled and narrowed his eyes at Clint but that only seemed to amuse the jerk.

Clint sloppily spun, then bowed and stumbled.

Machoponi found himself wondering if Clint's bumbling was completely on purpose. Clint probably had only a few more moments before he could no longer play off the ill effects of being on the dark side. Macho knew what he had to do.

34

And so, he pleaded, trying to seem as sincere as possible. "Please don't, Clint. It hurt so much when I crossed the line. I only pretended to be tough."

Clint sneered. "So I guess you're a *lot* less tough than me, you sissy!"

All the guys snickered. And the way Dust was looking at Macho, it almost seemed like she wanted to roll her eyes.

Macho said, "Okay, Clint, so you proved your point. Now come on back."

Clint replied, "Yeah, that's right, I proved that you may be the only poni with a blue ball in the village," and he started swaggering back toward the Jagged Line, "but I'm the only one in the village with brass ones," he said as he lifted his hoof over, just about to cross the line.

But as Macho was breathing a sigh of relief, Clint's tongue jutted out from his mouth, stuck in the "out" position, and he closed his eyes and raised his chin and performed a mocking ballet spin.

Macho shouted out, trying his best to sound meek, "Clint why are you doing this?"

Clint laughed and said, "Why?" as music began to play, and he began to sing this song:

Machoponi

You've Got to Try

'Why?' you ask! 'Why oh why?'
Why, of course, to catch the maiden's eye!
And while you may be chicken,
Because you just might die,
I'm not too scared to cross the line,
Cuz I'm not too scared to try!

Oh, there are ponies out there,
Who do not even try!
They cower underneath their beds,
And then they wonder why?!
'Why don't the girls look back,
When I look them in the eye?!'
'Why oh why?'
Could it be you're scared to try?

Oh, you've got to keep on trying,
Even if you fail,
Even if you fall down,
Get up and try again!

So, heck, yeah, I crossed the line, you sissy!
I crossed the line, and more!
I crossed to prove that I'm just not a big ol' bore!

Lotus Rose

Not dumb or boring with a stupid little ball,
But big and strong and dangerous,
And not a lameo at all!

Sometimes you've got to go for it!
You've got to go and try!
Cuz if you don't, you won't succeed,
And then you'll wonder 'why??'

36

And even if you stumble, even if you fall,
As you lay dying, at least you will know,
That at least you're not some dorky sissy
With a dorky ball!

And that's why, you've got to try...even if you die!

But then everyone's eyes opened wide, because behind Clint, Darkeyes and his platoon were coming out of the front opening of the military tent. Their coats were dark gray, their tails and manes were scraggly and dirty silver, as was typical of the undead. They all stumbled out as if half drunk.

And Clint seemed unaware of them!

Darkeyes was the replacement of the former leader of the platoon. He used to live in Macho's village when they were younger. When Darkeyes had crossed over into the dark side, he had stood forlornly for a

Machoponi

whole day, and everyone had wished he'd go away. He'd disappeared for a couple years, then returned to take the old leader's place. The first thing he did as the new leader was move the tent closer to the Jagged Line, as if to mock the pastel ponies. Darkeyes had adopted his own unique hairstyle since he'd become undead—his mane stuck up like two devil horns.

Darkeyes strutted as he and the other undead ponies walked toward Clint. Macho shouted out, "Clint! Darkeyes is behind you!" and as he said that the undead ponies began to grin, and Darkeyes shook his head slightly and made a face.

But Clint laughed mockingly! "Let him come!" he proclaimed.

Did he think it was all a joke? Macho wondered if Clint could actually be that stupid.

Clint pumped his front legs up and down while making a goofy face, then hopped to the side in a flourished motion, mimicking ballet movements. Behind him, Darkeyes and his crew playfully rocked their heads from side to side—two of them spun around.

And the platoon of undead crept closer. Macho

looked pleadingly to Dust. Surely she would say something, not wanting to see Clint harmed! But she just stood with a quirky grin on her face.

38

Now the seriousness of the situation sunk in to the members of Clint's clique and they began shouting things like, "I'm not kidding dude! He's right behind you! Hurry up and cross back over!"

But Clint laughed and went, "La la la, I love ballet!" Then he closed his eyes and performed another ballet spin. Behind him, the undead soldiers made goofy faces and struggled to laugh without making noise.

Clint opened his eyes to look back at Macho, Dust and the other guys.

A feeling of dread come over Macho. It was like Clint was dooming himself with his foolish behavior.

Behind him, the undead crept a few steps closer, then Clint began marching toward the edge of the Jagged Line—and Darkeyes watched with a scowl, but for some reason stood silently. But just as Clint was about to cross the line, his hoof froze in midair, hovering over the line, then Clint made a jerky dance movement, proclaimed, "Psyche!" then he began moonwalking backwards! With long graceful strides, he seemed to glide upon the earth, all to mock Macho. Clint glided backwards along the ground, then he backed right into Darkeyes! Their hooves thudded against each other and a cloud of dust plumed up.

Machoponi

Clint slowly lowered his head, took a pause, then uttered out the side of his mouth, "Hey Darkeyes." His voice was completely calm, which chilled Machoponi to the bone. And now Clint's expression turned into a vicious scowl as he turned around to face Darkeyes.

And Darkeyes' face showed fear!

Machoponi could hardly believe it, and he looked around at everyone around him—their faces showed complete surprise as well.

39

Clint made a noise in his throat that almost sounded like a growl, then shouted at Darkeyes, "Best step up off me!" Clint took a threatening step forward, and Darkeyes actually took a step back! "That's right," Clint said, then he twitched forward in a threatening manner. Darkeyes flinched! And behind him, the other undead ponies all looked scared! Clint chuckled, then continued to Darkeyes, "I oughta kick your ass right now, mofo! Then I oughta drag you back across the line and let you melt!"

Darkeyes lowered his head, then muttered, "Please don't hurt me. Please, just go. We don't want any trouble."

"I oughta knock you upside the head so hard, you have to walk on two legs the rest of your life!" The ponies of his clique chuckled. "And I also oughta—" But then Clint stopped talking and wobbled a little.

Darkeyes tilted his head and peered at him,

asking, "Yes?"

Clint's voice seemed strained as he said, "I'm gonna let you go now." He turned back around. "You're lucky," he said through a tight mouth.

He started walking shakily toward the Pastel Kingdom. He took two wobbly steps, then his knees buckled as he grunted and fell over.

Everyone on the pastel side gasped and a few of Clint's friends rushed toward the line, as if to cross, but then stopped.

40

All the undead gathered around Clint and looked down, then Darkeyes huffed in amusement and said, "Do *try* to get up, will you?" Clint didn't seem to be moving.

Machoponi found himself running across the line, seemingly without his conscious decision—all he knew was that he had to save Clint!

Macho charged forward and nudged one of the undead aside from behind, then stood defiantly staring at Darkeyes. Darkeyes met Macho's gaze with silence, which was surprising. But Macho didn't stop to question—instead, he switched into action mode. He said to Clint, "Clint can you hear me? You need to get up if you can."

But Clint was barely even conscious. The only thing that happened was that his head nudged slightly toward the sound of Macho's voice.

Machoponi

Macho looked at Darkeye's face, trying to read him...and Darkeyes looked back...and nodded.

Macho gestured with his jaw over to his blue ball over on the pastel side, then said, "Can you help me get Clint's forelegs up onto the ball? That way we can roll him across."

Darkeyes nodded. One of the guy ponies nudged the ball over the edge. Darkeyes then issued an order for his troops: "Blaine, lift up his mane. Rock, Butch, lift up his front."

And so they jumped into action, and using their combined efforts, they managed to lift and push Clint's unconscious front half onto Macho's blue ball. Clint had passed out at this point. Macho almost felt like passing out himself. He maneuvered himself behind Clint and pushed with his muzzle on Clint's bottom half. The undead soldiers helped to guide the rolling ball as it gained momentum. It was actually working! The smooth plastic ball rolled over and over underneath Clint's coat...and then Clint had made it across, followed shortly by Macho himself.

Macho turned back around to face the Dark Kingdom. Clint slid off the ball and plopped over onto the ground.

Macho bowed to the undead soldiers. "Thank you for helping me," he said.

Darkeyes acted like he didn't even hear it, and

turned around, then Darkeyes and the troops started walking back toward their tent.

Meanwhile, behind him, Macho thought he heard a very quiet word muttered to him: "Slushy."

He turned around and looked down at where the voice was coming from.

"What?" Macho said to Clint, truly puzzled. Clint looked up at him weakly from the ground, and with complete contempt, repeated, "Sissy."

42

Dust Gets in Your Eyes

Two days later, Dust came to visit Macho while he was laying sick in his bed.

At first, he felt elated when his mother brought Dust inside the house. But then, a feeling of disappointment came over him as he realized that Dust might simply not have anything better to do without Clint around. Clint hadn't been seen at all after the incident. His family said that he was off visiting distant family members. All the members of his clique said he was off cuddling with a girlponi, and practicing his dancing to come back to beat Machoponi in the upcoming dance off at the Promenade in a week. But no one else in the village seemed really sure exactly where Clint had gone.

Machoponi looked into Dust's eyes and she grinned at him gently, filling Macho with an array of confusing emotions and causing his heart to quicken.

Macho's mother looked back and forth between their gazes. Macho caught the sneer that flashed briefly across his mother's face, which Dust apparently didn't catch.

Macho's mother made a smacky noise with her mouth, then said in a sugary-sweet voice tinged with annoyance, "I'll leave you two to talk, but you can only stay for a few minutes. He needs his rest." Then she turned and left the room.

Machoponi didn't know what to say. He felt shy in front of Dust as she gazed at him, as she tilted her head, and her mane shifted fetchingly over her right eye.

44

Macho shifted his gaze to the ceiling, then nervously pulled his baby-blue blanky up higher on his body.

With a concerned tone, Dust asked, "Are you okay?"

"I've been better," Macho said, followed by a grin that resembled more of a grimace. "I just need another day or so, that's all."

"Well, I've been really worried about you."

Macho lowered his gaze and tried to read Dust's face. He couldn't believe what he was hearing. He said, "Really?"

Dust nodded. "Mmm hmm."

"Well, thank you for your concern. How's Clint doing?"

"They tell me he's fine and is visiting family. I think he's still recovering though."

Macho nodded.

Machoponi

Dust said, "I have something I've been wanting to tell you, and with Clint out of town, this will be the best chance I'll have for a while."

"Yes? What is it?"

Dust started fidgeting and could not meet his eyes. "I-I'm just gonna say it, and hope you don't hate me."

45

"Okay, please tell me."

After a long pause, Dust said, "I have feelings for you."

Macho was shocked.

Dust continued. "I hid it for a long time. I thought it was just a crush. Like, remember when you were a colt and I was a filly? I had a crush on you back then."

Macho chuckled. "Yes, I remember." Macho had a crush on Dust back then too, except *his* crush had never really gone away. Now they were both sixteen years old and things weren't the same.

Dust laughed then said, "Remember how I used to kiss you on the mouth, then run away?"

Macho grinned, "And I would chase you."

"Yeah, you used to say how gross it was!"

"But I was just a kid." Macho looked down shyly. "Actually, I kind of started liking it. But then you stopped."

46

"Well, I was just a kid too. I moved onto other guys. I guess I didn't realize what kind of guy you'd turn out to be."

"What kind of guy do you think I am?"

Her face took on a dreamy expression. "A very strong, very macho, but also a very kind and sensitive poni, and hopefully...loyal?" She looked at him timidly.

Macho hoped she was inferring what he thought she was. Macho's yearning for Dust was no secret in the village and was even the butt of many jokes. He'd never extinguished the flame in his heart ever since they were little kids. "Yes," he answered and his voice shook with emotion.

"Maybe we could have something good together. We have a lot of history. You have stuck up for me ever since we were kids. You've always been so kind to me. Maybe I need a kind guy. I don't know what that's like. You see, I've been wanting to break up with Clint for quite a while now. I've just been waiting for the right moment."

Macho tried hard to keep his voice calm, as he

asked, "Are you going to do it soon?"

A wicked grin crept up the side of Dust's face. "Yes, right after the Promenade. Think about how humiliating that would be." She chuckled, and despite himself, Macho chuckled too.

He said, "That sounds kind of mean."

"But it's what he deserves, don't you think?"

"Maybe so," Macho replied.

"And I'm sure you'll win in the dance off. Clint dances like he has four left hooves!"

Macho grinned.

47

"And right after you win, I'll break up with Clint right in front of everyone! That'll show him. But I had another thing I wanted to ask you about."

"Yes?"

"Clint's sister, you know her right? His oldest sister...."

"You mean Badunkadunk? Yes, I know her. I say hi to her every once in a while. What about her?"

"Well, this is going to sound strange, but right before the dance off, she wants to kiss you. Like a real kiss...on the mouth."

Macho was dumbfounded. "But why?"

"She hates her brother too and we've been planning this thing together. And you have to do it in front of everyone too. It will really tick Clint off! Imagine how he'll feel about you kissing his sister!"

Macho suddenly felt overwhelmed and was reminded of how ill he felt.

"But why?" he stammered. "What about you and me?"

Dust chuckled. "Don't worry. I'm not the jealous type. Besides, I know there's nothing between you two."

Macho opened his mouth to speak, but Dust put on her sad eyes and batted her long lashes irresistibly. "Please," she said. "It would mean so much to both of us."

48

"Okay," Macho said, weakly.

Dust seemed lost in thought for a moment, then chuckled.

"What?" Macho asked, grinning simply because she was.

"Remember that time by the pond back when I would kiss you and run away? You were looking at a butterfly one day...."

Macho shook his head.

"Well," she said. "I thought you were so cute, how intensely you were staring at that butterfly. And I crept beside you and I kissed the side of your mouth."

"And then you ran away?"

"Yes, and you chased me and tripped and fell..."

Suddenly Macho remembered. "I was crying," he said, "and you were laughing at me!"

"I didn't know what I was doing back then. But I thought you were so cute with your pouty little face and

Machoponi

your vulnerability."

"Then you stuck your tongue out at me!" Macho shouted in mock anger.

"Because you didn't catch me."

"Maybe someday I will," Macho said.

"Maybe someday soon I'll kiss you again...."

"Will you run away?"

"We'll see...."

Then, after saying goodbye, Dust left Macho alone with his thoughts.

It took Machoponi three days to recover. It generally took normal ponies four or five days to recover, but Machoponi was strengthened by his exceptional machismo.

During the next week, Machoponi practiced his dance moves. Half his time he devoted to the types of dances he did for the public—the kind that made ponies hoot in approval and shake their heads in disbelief. But the other half of his valuable practice time, he devoted to his love, his art, his calling...ballet. Why did ponies mock such beautiful movement of the body? Was it just because he was a male? Was it not macho?

Well, Macho knew better—he knew the truth. He had an ancient book from the Time When People Walked with Ponies. He couldn't read very well, but his great-grandfather could, and had read to Macho the name of the strong, very macho ballet dancer in the book,

who Macho gazed admiringly at nearly every day while practicing. The man's name was Mikhail Nikolaevitch Baryshnikov. And Baryshnikov was Macho's inspiration as he would close his eyes and perform the ballet spin and as he would reach for the sky in grand leaps like a gazelle.

50

The Promenade Begins!

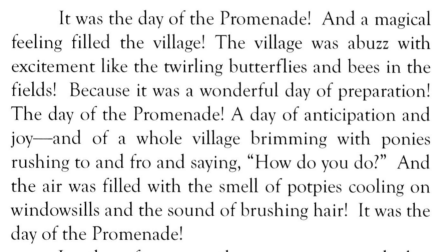

51

It was the day of the Promenade! And a magical feeling filled the village! The village was abuzz with excitement like the twirling butterflies and bees in the fields! Because it was a wonderful day of preparation! The day of the Promenade! A day of anticipation and joy—and of a whole village brimming with ponies rushing to and fro and saying, "How do you do?" And the air was filled with the smell of potpies cooling on windowsills and the sound of brushing hair! It was the day of the Promenade!

In the afternoon, there even appeared that smile-upside-down called a rainbow, stretching its back between the two kingdoms. It usually only showed itself a couple of times a month, and here it was to mark the grand day. The half that was inside the Pastel Kingdom, was colorfully ROYGBIV, and the half that crossed into the Dark Kingdom was in shades of gray, just like always.

How comforting it was to see it return the same as

it always did, for, like the comforting stars, it was always the same, but unlike them, it did not appear every day. But it appeared this day, because this day was a day of yummy goodness, a day like the cream inside a chocolate cupcake mixing with the icing outside!

"Are you ready?" they'd ask each other, then laugh because no one could wait! Because it was the glorious, fantastic, gleefully gay day of

52

THE PROMENADE

Finally the nighttime arrived, the stars came out and began to twinkle like unscratched plastic!

The drawbridge of the Purple Castle lowered to welcome the entrance of the party-going ponies! The crowd cheered! They began to file into the castle. And Oh, what a glorious spectacle they were!

The girlponies were first, each wearing a tiara sparkling with shimmering clear plastic and a large red plastic jewel heart as its centerpiece. Dust led the group, because she had been proclaimed Princess for a Day. Some said that *all* the girlponies were equally beautiful and since they each wore a tiara, that "every poni is a princess," but of course, that's crap. They all wore luxurious gowns of velvet and silk and colors like red and purple. O, how deliciously sinful it was to wear clothing, just like the fabled humans from days of old!

Machoponi

Upon the dainty forelegs of each fine maiden, clung striped legwarmers of all colors of the rainbow. All the proper colors that is—not gray. Because gray was not allowed in the pastel side. And they marched in lockstep into the castle and to the ballroom inside!

Now the guy ponies began filing in over the drawbridge! And they were dressed handsomely with a top hat upon each masculine head and a fuchsia boa wrapped around each strong neck.

To the ballroom they went!

The ballroom was a glorious room. Large and luxurious—from the inside it almost seemed larger than the castle itself! They all entered the room by the wooden banisters at the top of the two winding staircases, the guys on the left side of the room and the girls on the right.

53

The two long staircases led down to the central dance floor which was made of checkered black and white marble. Above it twinkled a large ornate chandelier. Machoponi was in front of the line of guys and he pushed his blue ball down the staircase, which ploomped ploomped down then bounced into the beautiful water fountain in the center of the floor.

And guess what was swishing inside that fountain?

Floating to and fro like darting tadpoles were three merponies happily playing with the borrowed beachball! (Merponies have the heads of ponies and

the bodies of fish.)

Making her entrance, at the front of the line of girlponies, was Dust, the Princess for a Day. She looked around dramatically and grinned and proclaimed,

"Let the Promenade begin!"

Everyone cheered, "Hooray!"

With a glint in his eye, Machoponi looked across the room, enthralled at Dust's dimpled smile. Macho and Dust began slowly leading everyponi down the staircases as the merponies began to sing:

Shoopy shoopy doo shoop shoopa shoopy doo

Then music began to play and all the girlponies started to sing this song:

It's Fun to Put on a Dress

"Oh, it's fun to put on a dress!
To revel in sweet excess!"

Dust looked over at the guys and winked with modelesque smile. A couple of the guys stumbled because she was so beautiful.

(The guys and girls were now 3/4 of the way down the staircases.)

Dust called to the guys, "Oh, ain't it fun to put on a dress?!"

At which the guys shouted back: "We guess!"

Machoponi

And the girlponies shouted back, "You guess?!!" before they started to sing again while continuing down the stairs,

"Ohhhh...it's fun to put on a dress,
When you're feeling a little burlesque,
Cuz naked is boring and normal,
And doesn't take as much finesse!"
The guys shouted back, "We guess!"

Now Dust stood on the landing in the middle of the staircase. Macho and Clint both stood on the landing opposite her, waiting.

55

Dust sang,
"Well, you don't understand I suppose,
Just how wonderful and sexy are clothes,
And I suppose that you won't be impressed,
With my choice of fine fashion unless...."
Clint and Macho shouted out, "What?"
"Unless I let you...."
"Yeah?!" all the guys shouted back.
"...Unless I let you look up my dress!"

She then turned around fetchingly on the landing, beckoning with her hindquarters. The guys immediately knew what to do. They rushed madly down the stairs to find that glorious angle where they could look up Dust's dress. Their jaws dropped. It was a glorious sight, greater than any painting from the days of yore—a work of art.

A few of the guyponie's' top hats even fell off as they strained their necks to see.

And the merponies looked on with envy and one even muttered sarcastically, "What an ass!" then mocked Dust by sticking her own tail out of the water at the guys.

56

But Dust only grinned, then shouted back at the merponi with sugary sweetness, "What a nice tail! And what did you say?"

And the merponi, taken aback, shouted, "What a nice ass you are!"

And Dust shouted back, "I'm not an ass, but a poni! And you still have a beautiful tail!"

The merponi blushed at the compliment, then swam around the fountain with a big grin.

Dust put on a smile and began to sing again as she stepped down the last half of the staircase:

**"Sooo...when you're feeling a little burlesque,
It's nice to put on a dress!"**

Then the instruments stopped playing and everyone thought the song was over, but Dust started

singing a solo as she slowly walked down the final steps of the staircase.

This is what she sang:

Ohhh, but now I must confess...

"What???" everyone else shouted in unison.

I've got a secret, but you can't see...unless!...

"What???" Ponies looked at each other with bewilderment, then shifted their gazes back onto Dust. "Will you show us?"

"Ohhhhh...I'll show you my secret I guess, but you can't see, no you can't see unless..."

Everyone else shouted, "Unless??!"

"Yes! You can't see unleeeeess. I said you can't see, you can't see unleeeeee..."

57

The room took a collective gasp of anticipation as Dust took the last step onto the dance floor while holding one note. Her voiced started shifting into a higher pitch as she turned her backside toward all the girlponies.

"...eeeeessss

You look up my dress!"

And with those words Dust applied a powerful booty quake motion which caused the bottom half of her dress to lift up and fold over her back, so that her rear was exposed for everypony to see.

Then they all stood contemplating Dust's naked bottom, the best one in the village.

Lotus Rose

And the guys on the left side of the room began gasping and exclaiming in surprise, while the girls were silent and calm because they were at the wrong angle to see what the guys saw.

One of the guyponies shouted out, "A tramp stamp! She has a tramp stamp!"

And it was true! There, on her flank, above her right leg for all the guyponies and merponies to see was a new tattoo of a red heart-outline inside a black circle. And running jaggedly down the center of the heart was her scar.

And as the room filled with shocked murmurs, Macho watched the huge grin form on Dust's face.

The Promenade

59

Dust's mocking laughter echoed throughout the dance hall. She said, "Well you've been staring at my butt quite long enough!" She made a little butt jiggle motion to emphasize her point. "But now that you've got a good gander, and my dress you have now looked *quite* under..." She giggled. "...it's time to move on to what we came here for: to dance dance dance!" Then she twitched her back to flip her dress over and cover her rear.

All the ponies began cheering at the mention of dancing. They all filed down the stairs onto the dance floor. They lined up so the guys were on the left side of the room and the girls were on the right, and each guyponi faced a girlponi partner. The classical waltz music began to play, heavy on the string instruments. Then each couple began gracefully walking toward each other. Macho was across from Badunkadunk, with her beautiful pink hair with white stripes and her light-blue body. Dust was across from Clint, and that made

Macho really jealous.

All the couples stopped in the middle of the room, a couple of feet away from each other and bowed gracefully as the beautiful music filled the air. They danced the rest of the moves to the music: they circled each other by stepping forward to pass their partner's side, then walking sideways, then stepping backwards, then stepping to the side so that they faced their partner again, then they bowed.

60

That was how it started. Then they would begin to dance in their own way, with the guy leading. Sometimes the pairs would do dance steps to the side, or forward or backward. Some couples even touched their muzzles together, and occasionally a girl would spin. Then the music would end, so they would walk backward away from each other, then bow. Then they would either stand on the edges of the room, socializing, or line up for another dance. The evening continued on this way, until it was almost time for the dance off.

It was a few minutes before the scheduled dance off and Macho was trying his best to relax. He knew he had nothing to worry about, because he'd been practicing for weeks, plus he was clearly a much better dancer than Clint. Macho was more nervous about the kiss he was supposed to have with Badunkadunk.

He was standing on the edge of the dance floor watching the ponies dance.

Machoponi

He heard someone say, "Pssst" into his right ear. He turned his head to see Dust smiling at him.

"Hey handsome," she said.

"Hey beautiful," Macho replied.

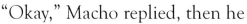

Dust batted her lashes. "I want to speak to you a little bit before you do that dance off." She motioned with her head toward a hallway.

"Okay," Macho replied, then he

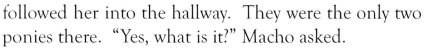

followed her into the hallway. They were the only two ponies there. "Yes, what is it?" Macho asked.

"Well...I just couldn't *bear* to have Badunkadunk kiss you before...I had a chance to kiss you myself." She moved her mouth toward his and Macho leaned forward too. Their mouths touched and Macho's heart quickened. Then he felt Dust's tongue pressing to touch his and their tongues mingled. Then Macho was suddenly stuck by a strange sensation. His tongue felt like it was tingling and becoming cold. Dust pulled back and Macho stared into her beautiful eyes. What was that chilly feeling? Was that what love felt like?

Dust giggled, then said, "There, I kissed you first. You're mine."

Macho felt the blush rising in his cheeks.

Dust smiled. "Now go have an interesting dance

off, baby."

"Thank you," Macho stammered, then he turned to walk back. As he went back onto the dance floor, he saw Badunkadunk standing ahead of him, to the right. She was facing the opposite direction. A few moments later, Dust came up behind him, then went off to mingle in the crowd.

It was almost time for the dance off and Macho felt himself feeling a little dizzy from anticipation. The waltz music stopped and someone shouted, "It's time for the dance off!" The murmurs spread throughout the room.

Across the room, Macho saw Clint making his way through the crowd. Macho's legs began to feel weak. Badunkadunk was turning around to face him.

Macho began walking closer to Badunkadunk. She grinned at him. As he came up to her, she said, "You're a stud, Macho," and she tilted her head and puckered up. Nervously, Macho kissed her. He had only meant it to be a short kiss, but as he tried to pull back, Badunkadunk pressed forward and slipped him some tongue. Their tongues touched and Macho was surprised to feel his tongue tingling with a chill! What was this strange cold feeling? It was like when he'd kissed Dust! He didn't understand and he began to sway with confusion as he pulled his mouth away from Badunkadunk's.

Machoponi

He searched the room for Dust, then he saw her about thirty feet away. He wanted to read her expression to make sure she had meant it when she'd said she wouldn't mind him kissing Badunkadunk.

He made eye contact with her. And then Dust shouted out in alarm, "How could you?"

The surprise hit Macho so hard that it made his head spin. Dust began crying out loud.

Macho shouted at her, "Dust wait!" but for some reason, he slurred his words. Clumsily, he tried to walk toward her.

But Dust yelled, "Don't come near me! Go do your dance contest! You'll learn your lesson afterwards!" She stared hatefully at him, and Macho stood with all the ponies' eyes on him, and the effect of everything was now making him woozy.

He looked to his right and Clint was standing next to him. Clint sneered and said, "Did you have fun kissing my sister? We'll talk about that later. Now, let's dance."

Macho nodded and hoped his shakiness would disappear once he started dancing.

Macho turned to face Clint, then they each stepped backward so that they weren't too close to each other. Then the music began to play.

The song was a recording of an old school rap by the band, Run P.O.Knee, and it was called:

It's Spiffy

The opening music of the song filled the dance hall as Clint and Macho stared each other down and made mean faces at each other. Macho was finding it difficult to focus, though, for some reason. They each flung off their top hats and boas.

64

And Run P.O.Knee began their rap:

I met this little poni, the color macaroni.
Said she could really dance,
But she turned out to be a phony.
I met another filly, she said I looked real silly,
But then I pranced around for her,
And now she's on my willy.

(Then the chorus started and Clint and Macho began dancing frantically as Run P.O.Knee rapped:)

It's spiffy to prance in time, to prance in time, that's
    right, equine.
It's spiffy!... It's spiffy spiffy spiffy spiffy.

Macho was doing some elaborate footwork, at least he was trying to. He was having some trouble

warming up. He stumbled a little.

Across from him, Clint was popping-and-locking, which was a style of dance where he seemed to jolt into sudden movement then freeze, then move again. He was jerking his head from side to side and alternately lifting his legs and stepping down.

As the second verse began, Clint began jutting his chest out while bouncing up and down.

Macho leaned forward, preparing to go onto his back and spin on the floor, but instead he lost his balance and fell over.

And Run P.O.Knee rapped:

65

And in this poni world, it's always so pastel,
And gray they say is not allowed, and it's like hell,
Cuz hell is when you can't be sad or who you are,
And now I say they took pastel just way too far.

It's spiffy to prance in time...

The music came to a sudden stop.

Macho was feeling really dizzy and could barely lift his head off the floor. He opened one eye to look at Clint—Clint had stopped dancing and was laughing at him!

Someone was walking toward Macho. He thought he recognized the hooves and he managed to raise his

eyes. Dust was standing in front of him. He tried to speak, but for some reason he couldn't even begin to form words.

"How could you?" Dust shouted down at him. "First you cheat on me by kissing another girl and then you get drunk for such an important event? You've broken my heart, Macho, I hope you know that!" She looked around at the entire room of watchers. "I hope everyone knows that! I can't live on, knowing what he's done to me!"

66

There was a collective gasp through the room.

And Macho felt horribly confused and wanted to speak, to tell her that he wasn't drunk. He had no idea what was wrong with him, but something was definitely wrong. And he desperately wanted to ask Dust why she was saying such things when the kiss with Badunkadunk had been Dust's idea in the first place!

Macho tried to say, "What are you saying?" but the words wouldn't come to Macho's mouth—instead he slurred out, "Wha—wha—whaut."

Badunkadunk shouted at Dust, "I didn't know that Macho was still with you, Dust! He told me he wasn't involved with you anymore! He lied to me! You've got to believe me!"

Macho shook his head in disbelief. What was happening? Why was Badunkadunk lying? He'd *never* been involved with Badunkadunk at all!

Machoponi

Dust replied to Badunkadunk, "I believe you. I'm not angry at you at all. I just feel so hurt. We were both fooled by Macho."

Clint, who was now standing beside Badunkadunk, shouted at Dust, "You cheated on me, but maybe we can work this out. Don't do anything drastic."

"No," Dust replied. "I can never get over Macho's betrayal. He convinced me to cheat on you, then he ended up cheating on *me*! I've lost all faith in him. He's no good. You broke my heart, Macho."

Macho's eyes widened in horror. How could this be happening!

67

Dust stared at Macho for a couple seconds, then burst into tears and galloped out of the dance hall. Badunkadunk followed her out.

A few guys started to gallop after her, but Clint shouted out, "Stop! It would be the worst thing you could do right now, if you followed her! Let her go!" so the ponies who had been following Dust stopped. Clint then said, "Give her a few moments to calm down, then I will talk to her. I hope she'll get over what Macho did to her." Clint's voice sounded filled with concern.

Shakily, Macho attempted to stand and managed to get back on his four hooves again. He seemed to be feeling a little less dizzy. A twinkle caught his attention. He looked down to see Dust's tiara lying on the floor. One of his friends asked if he was okay, and Macho

managed to say, "I don't know."

He looked over at Clint. Some guyponies were talking to him, trying to convince him to go after Dust or to at least let one of them go to her. Clint was shaking his head, and saying, "No, I'm her boyfriend. I know her. Leave her alone for a while."

And so everyponi stood awkwardly in silence. Then slowly, ponies began to engage in conversations. And Macho continued to feel less dizzy. Many of the other ponies seemed to be avoiding him—some of them glared at him.

Machoponi only stared ahead with a glum expression on his face.

Suddenly, Badunkadunk rushed into the room, screaming, "Hurry! It's Dust! She just fell over! I think she's died of a broken heart!"

Everyone rushed outside and followed Badunkadunk. Macho was swept along with the rest of the crowd. He was relieved that he was no longer dizzy.

Badunkadunk led them a short distance outside the castle. It was dark outside, but the moon was full and provided some light.

They could see a poni lying on the ground and it looked like Dust. And as the crowd of ponies got closer, they could see, under the light of the moon, that it was indeed her.

68

Machoponi

Clint and Badunkadunk, who were leading the crowd, stopped in their tracks. Then, various ponies started shouting at Dust, but she didn't move.

But Macho was pushing his way through the crowd. He was going to revive Dust—he *had* to.

Beside him, Badunkadunk was yelling, "You broke her heart, and now she's dead!" as Macho leaned down and felt for Dust's pulse on her neck with his mouth.

With dread, he realized she had no pulse.

"Come back, Dust!" he shouted through tears. For several minutes, he shouted and cried.

69

But Dust never revived. As the realization that she was truly gone struck Macho, he felt overwhelming sorrow. He didn't know how he could live without her in his life. She was the only girl he'd ever loved.

And Macho took a few steps backward, as the dizziness suddenly overwhelmed him once again. Helplessly, he watched Dust's body lying still on the ground—watched as darkness filled his eyes, and Macho took a few more steps backward before collapsing.

Oh, Dust. You have left me, he thought, just before he closed his eyes and everything went black.

Even in Death

70

Machoponi awoke in darkness. It felt like he was lying down on the ground. He looked around, tried to focus. He saw hooves he didn't recognize. One of the hooves rested on top of a blue ball that looked an awful lot like Macho's. He tried to lift his head and saw Clint's face.

Clint said to him, "You died. The official cause of death was a broken heart."

Macho struggled to make sense of Clint's words.

Clint continued, "You're on the dark side now. They were going to hold a funeral for you, but that isn't going to happen now. The village doesn't really like you much now, anyway. I wonder if anyone would show up."

Macho shook his head and tried to stand up. "Why?" he asked.

"Look," Clint said, "those undead poni jerks took Dust and it's not right. You have to bring her back. You

were already dead so I took the opportunity to push your body over the line. You're reanimated. You can do this now. You *have* to do this! Bring her back."

Macho finally managed to stand. He felt overwhelmed by what Clint was telling him.

Clint said, "Believe it. Look around you. You're in the Dark Kingdom."

Macho turned and looked around. The grass under his feet was brown and everything looked murkier around him. He looked at Clint who seemed to be surrounded by pastel colors (although they were darker because it was still dark outside.) Everything Clint said seemed to be true. It was a shock to suddenly realize that he was dead. He didn't want to believe it. "What do you mean, they took Dust? They reanimated her?"

71

"Yes. They somehow got hold of her body. She reanimated and they kidnapped her!"

Macho was shocked. "Why? What are they going to do with her?"

Clint gestured at a rolled up piece of parchment lying on the ground. "My grandfather had an ancient map of the dark side of Poniworld, from the time before the Great Dividing, when the Dark Kingdom was still pastel. You can use it to guide your path. The undead ponies are taking Dust to the castle where the Princess of the Dark Kingdom dwells. I don't know what route they're using, but the map shows that there is a large

chasm in front of the castle and there is only one way to cross: a rope bridge. You have to get to that rope bridge before the undead ponies do. You can head them off. All you have to do is get to the bridge first. They have about a four-hour lead. You can catch up with them if you don't sleep."

"What time is it?" Macho asked.

"It's almost dawn. And don't worry about the sun hurting you, since you're undead. It won't hurt you. That's just a myth, though the sun is much less bright on the dark side."

Macho struggled to take in all of Clint's words.

Clint continued, "Bring her back to me. You messed this up, now you have to fix it. We'll settle it when you come back, then Dust can decide between us—let the best poni win. If it means anything, she told me she loved you. I don't know why she did, though." Clint rolled the blue ball over to Macho, then he turned around, as if to end the conversation.

Macho asked, "How do you know they're taking her to the Princess of the Dark Kingdom?"

Without turning around, Clint said, "Darkeyes told me. They used to be lovers." Then Clint began to walk away, and he would no longer reply to anything Macho said.

Macho looked down at the rolled up parchment on the ground. It was yellow and old. The parchment

was attached to a string. The string was tied to two red, plastic gumball-looking balls which Macho figured were used to weigh the parchment down when it was opened.

The sun had begun to rise, providing light.

He kneeled down and nudged the parchment open. He used the plastic balls to hold the top and bottom of the parchment down.

73

The map was drawn simply and showed all of Poniworld. But there was no Jagged Line through the middle. On the bottom half of the parchment were all the major landmarks and villages of the Pastel Kingdom. On the upper half were all the things that used to be in the Dark Kingdom before it became dark. At the top of the map was a castle labeled, "The Princess's Castle." In front of it was the chasm with a single rope bridge drawn on it. The chasm went all the way from the left of the map to the right, and the bridge was the only way to cross that the map showed. It was just as Clint said.

He studied the map, trying to figure out a good path to the rope bridge. The two kingdoms had been divided so long ago, that no one remembered what the upper half of Poniworld was like, or what mysteries it held past the things in plain sight. He chose a path that looked like the shortest one: he would go through the Village of the Cuddlebears, then through Flutter-fly Poni Valley, then the Territory of the Chill-Aid

Man. The map showed a "yellow brick road" that went through all three areas. If he followed the road, he'd be less likely to get lost, he thought.

The map showed that on the top edge of the Chill-Aid Man's Territory was a wall that extended quite a distance to the left and right. The yellow brick road went right up to the wall, but the map didn't show a tunnel or door or anything. There were tunnels to the left and right, but they seemed far.

The rope bridge was on the other side of wall, very close to where the yellow-brick road met the wall. If he could figure out a way to go over the wall, he could save a lot of time. The map didn't indicate how high the wall was.

He didn't know if he was choosing a good path, or even if the map was accurate anymore, but he had no other information to go by, so it was the path he was going to take.

He stared at the map a few more minutes, committing it to memory in case something happened to it, then he rolled it up and slipped the string around his neck.

He headed toward the Village of the Cuddlebears.

The Village of the Cuddlebears

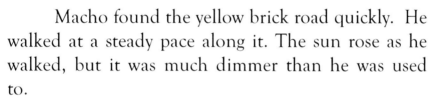

Macho found the yellow brick road quickly. He walked at a steady pace along it. The sun rose as he walked, but it was much dimmer than he was used to.

The map showed that a stream ran through the middle of the Cuddlebear Village. In the village, the yellow brick road went over a bridge that crossed the stream. He'd have to go over the bridge, because he couldn't swim and, on the map, there were no other bridges indicated nearby.

The word "cuddlebears" sounded pleasant and cuddly. It wasn't what he expected from the Dark Kingdom. He wondered if the cuddlebears were still there. Maybe the undead ponies had run them off or even destroyed them. It would be fine, though, if the village was deserted. Macho wanted as little trouble as possible in his voyage.

He had walked for about two hours when from a distance he could see a village made up of gray cottages

and eight gray animals walking around. They didn't look like bears, though.

As he got closer, he realized they had quills! They gathered into the center of the village, in front of the bridge that went over the stream, and watched him approach.

Well, there's no chance of passing through unnoticed now, Macho thought.

He stopped in front of the crowd. There were eight of the creatures, all male. He figured that they were porcupines, but they didn't look like regular ones. Their facial features actually resembled bears and they were bigger than normal porcupines—they were almost the same size as Macho.

One of the creatures asked, "Who are you, poni? Why aren't you gray like the rest?"

Macho thought that maybe it would be better to lie. "My name is Machoponi, and I dyed my hair," he said.

"Why?"

Macho thought briefly for a good lie. "The Princess told me to. I'm not sure why. I just did what she told me."

The one who was asking Macho the questions seemed to be considering whether to believe him, then he said, "I think you're from the Pastel Kingdom and you haven't been undead long enough for your hair to

76

Machoponi

turn gray. I've seen a couple others before, like you."

"Okay," Macho replied. "Yes, I'm from the pastel side."

"I thought so. Well, hello, my name is TooCool. Wanna know why they call me TooCool?"

"Sure."

"Because I'm too cool to care."

"Ah."

"That's a nice ball," said TooCool. "So what are you doing here? And is that a map around your neck?"

Macho nodded. He decided to lie again. "Yes. I want to meet the Princess and I'm using the map to guide me."

"You want to kill the Princess?"

Macho shook his head. "No, no, of course not."

TooCool peered at him. "You better not. I've noticed that the ponies who were recently reanimated take a while before the dark side converts them to the *right* way of thinking. It seems a lot of pastel ponies think they're supposed to be good and nice and maybe sometimes they think they should overthrow the Princess as a good deed. They are mistaken, you see. But it doesn't take long for them to be transformed, and once their hair turns completely gray and silver, their thoughts have changed too. But until that time, ponies like *you* can't be trusted. I've never seen a poni with a ball like

77

yours though. That's a nice ball. Us cuddlebears can't play with balls, because we always pop them."

Without thinking, Macho proudly said, "My ball is protected by a spell that keeps it from ever being popped." As soon as he said it, he realized he shouldn't have. The creatures glanced at each other, while Macho asked, "Did you say you were cuddlebears? Is this the Village of the Cuddlebears?"

"Yes."

"But on the pastel side, bears don't have spikes. Forgive me, this is new for me."

"Oh, we cuddlebears have had quills ever since the dark side became dark and we became undead. Before that, we were cute and cuddly and squishy and... bleh! Sickening. Did you know, that back in the old days, us cuddlebears even had something known as the 'Cuddlebear Stare'?"

Macho shook his head. "I don't know much about your half of Poniworld."

"Well," said the cuddlebear, "We had this thing called the Cuddlebear Stare, but it was stupid, because it didn't even come from our eyes at all! You see, each cuddlebear had a symbol on their stomach of a heart inside a circle, and when we did the Cuddlebear Stare, light would shoot out of the symbol and if you got hit by the light, it would make you want to be nice and care about others. It was completely stupid! I'm glad

those days are over. Now, our tummies are covered in quills. Now we each have a symbol of a corruptagram, but it doesn't matter, because you can't see it. We can still do a version of the Cuddlebear Stare though, but it's different. And we call it the Cuddlebear Flare. It's more accurate, don't you think?"

Macho nodded. "How is it different?"

"Well it makes you not care about anything at all. But nevermind that. I've been admiring your ball this whole time. Like I said, we can't play with balls, because we pop them. We have to use round rocks instead." He pouted and looked utterly miserable.

79

Macho was starting to feel disturbed by the way the cuddlebears were looking at his ball. It seemed that they were longing for it. "Errr," Macho said. "You wouldn't enjoy my ball much. It doesn't really bounce. It's the price of the spell. It won't pop, but it won't bounce either. Ironic, aye?" He desperately hoped they would believe his lie.

TooCool arched his brow. "I dunno. It looks like a pretty bouncy ball to me."

"No to the bouncy bouncy. Only plut plut," Macho said, trying to recreate the sound of a non-bouncing, flat ball.

The cuddlebears were approaching closer.

TooCool said, "I'd like to sing a song."

"No song," Macho replied. "I mean, I don't think

this occasion deserves a song. I'll just be on my way. Nice meeting you. You all seem pretty cool."

TooCool announced, "This song, though it is not specifically about you, is a classic that is still relevant, for you are from the pastel side and we are from the dark. And though the song is a traditional love song, it is not without its parallels to you and I, purple poni. It goes a little something like this:"

"Please don't," Macho whispered. He didn't understand many of the words TooCool had used, but it all sounded bad.

But the cuddlebear continued to sing this song as all the cuddlebears began advancing on Machoponi:

All those days and nights,
We were so far apart.
Remembering all those days before,
When you had pierced my heart.
And here you are now standing so close to me,
I wanna hug you and hold you so cuddly.

It's such a pleasure to say,
Two cuds for you!!
Two cuds for yoooooooo!!!

In one motion the cuddlebears all rose onto their hind legs, standing upright, holding their front legs out,

80

Machoponi

baring their tummies of quills, ready to pierce Macho with their horrible cuddles that kill!

Macho really wanted to pounce and bludgeon TooCool with at least one solid blow, but he got too scared. He turned to gallop away, but then he stopped. He could have easily outrun the cuddlebears, but then he wouldn't be able to cross the bridge and continue on his journey to rescue Dust! He had to figure out a way past the cuddlebears.

He yelled out, "Wait!"

He thought for a moment, then an idea popped into his head. He turned around to face the cuddlebears, who were watching him curiously.

Macho tried his best to sound condescending, as he said, "You say you like my ball, but you sissies look like you wouldn't know what to do with a ball if you had one...." Then he laughed mockingly. "You have no balls!"

TooCool, who seemed to speak for the whole group, was outraged. "That's not true! We'd know what to do with it, and we'd play with it a lot better than you!"

All the cuddlebears went back down onto all fours.

Macho's plan was working. It seemed you could always get a guy to act foolishly if you insulted his pride. Macho smirked, then said, "Well, how about we play a game of hoofball and see about that? If I win, I keep my ball and you'll let me go forward in my journey. If you

81

82

win, you still let me go forward, but you can keep the ball. Unless you're too scared you'll lose? Is it a deal?" The cuddlebears glanced at each other, then nodded and agreed. Macho nudged the ball forward and began walking toward them. "So where do you usually play your games with your...rocks?"

TooCool said they usually played right there in front of the bridge. They said they didn't know how to play hoofball and were very curious about it.

Macho explained the rules of the game to them. It involved running back and forth, kicking the ball with your hooves and kicking the ball into a net. The cuddlebears didn't have nets, so they used stones to indicate the goals. They didn't have hooves either, so they would use their feet.

Macho asked them what sorts of games they usually played if they didn't know how to play hoofball.

"Well," said TooCool, "we have a game called rock roll, where we take the roundest rock we can find, even though it's usually a little lopsided. Then we take turns. One team rolls the rock from one end of the field to the other, while the other team calls them names. When they reach the end of the field, that's one point, then, they switch, and the other team rolls the rock. They keep doing that until one team gives up. Most of the time it's a tie, but sometimes a team wins. It depends on how tired everyone is."

Machoponi

Macho nodded when he heard of their game, then said, "That sounds great!" Inside his head, though, he was thinking, *I've never heard of a stupider game in all my life, except for maybe T-ball.*

But luckily, they were going to play hoofball.

"So," said TooCool, "how should we divide the teams? We usually do four on four. We used to have a lot more players before the Great Cuddle War—now us eight are the only ones left."

"Wait, what was the Great Cuddle War?" Macho asked.

"Oh, that. Well, there was a dispute over the score of a game of rock roll, so everyone started aggressively cuddling. It got out of control, and went on for a couple of years, and well, now there are only eight of us left. And there are no more girl cuddlebears, so we can no longer reproduce."

"What does reproduce mean?"

"It means to procreate. But nevermind that. Let's just play cuddlebears against ponies. The first team to three points wins."

So the players divided into their teams of ponies versus cuddlebears. So it was eight cuddlebears against one poni. One of the cuddlebears was the goalie of their team. Macho didn't have a goalie, or maybe *he* was the goalie.

And so, after Macho set his map on the ground, the

game began. It was almost embarrassingly easy for Macho. At the beginning of the game, Macho immediately took the ball from a cuddlebear's possession, then galloped to the end of the field, where he easily kicked the ball past the goalie to score a point. The ball bounced off a cottage after he scored.

"One point!" he shouted, while the cuddlebears mumbled about "luck."

It would be easy to win the game, he thought, then the cuddlebears would let him past and he would get to keep his ball and this part of the journey would be over with.

84

He had two more points to go before winning the game. A determined look crossed his face. He had to make sure not to get cocky. Even though their bear legs didn't seem to be very well-suited for playing hoofball, he didn't know what kind of tricks the cuddlebears might be hiding.

The goalie kicked the ball. Macho got possession of it, and after that, it was easy. As he galloped to the end of the field, he almost felt sorry for them. It must be horrible to be covered in quills, he thought, as he watched the cuddlebears clumsily running around the field and almost bumping into each other. Some of them had to make sudden jerky movements just to keep from colliding. He found himself worrying about them, because he didn't want them to get hurt or accidentally

impaled. He pouted.

"Two points!" Macho yelled as he scored another easy goal, and TooCool, who now seemed to be the leader of the opposite team, scowled.

Before the next play, all the cuddlebears got together in a huddle and whispered amongst themselves. Macho could not hear any of it.

They all positioned themselves for the next play. But before the goalie kicked the ball, all the cuddlebears rose up and stood on their hind legs.

They shouted out:

Cuddlebear Flare!

A chimey sound issued forth, then shining beams of light shot from their tummies and shined on Macho. He winced, but felt no pain or anything.

It didn't seem to hurt him, so he didn't care. "What the F?" he said. "I call foul."

"Hey," said TooCool, "you told us the rules and you said a foul involves touching, and we didn't touch you at all. Therefore, we didn't break any rules."

Macho shrugged. "Whatever. I don't care. All I know is that I gotta win this game. I don't know why it really matters, though. What does anything matter, really?"

TooCool chuckled. "Now you know firsthand what the Cuddlebear Flare does! It makes you not care."

Macho rolled his eyes, then replied, "So what?" He gave an intense stare to the cuddlebears, then crinkled his eyes and said, "I'm out of control! I don't give a flying F anymore! Let's play ball."

The cuddlebears looked a little confused by his words.

86

As Machoponi waited for the goalie to kick the ball, he realized that not only did he not give an F about this stupid game, but he no longer cared whether these moron cuddlebears skewered themselves like jumbo shrimps on a shishkabob, because he no longer cared about anyone's feelings.

Then a perverse idea popped into his head—he would trick the cuddlebears into running into each other! It's not like he cared so much one way or the other—it would just be so easy. And it might actually be kinda funny to watch the cuddlebears get hurt. He found his thoughts interesting—he never would have wanted to kill the cuddlebears if he was his normal self. If only he cared.

He purposefully lost the next two points. He toyed with the cuddlebears, making it seem like a challenge, but he was really just getting them used to chasing him around.

Machoponi

After each goal against him, Macho merely shrugged and said, "Whatever."

The cuddlebears, he figured, must have been glad that he no longer seemed to care enough to try to win.

Ah yes, the cuddlebears looked so smug. The score was tied 2 to 2.

At the start of the next play, Macho immediately got possession of the ball. This time, though, he ran all over the field with the ball, evading the cuddlebears and easily keeping the ball away from them. "Come on you sissies!" he shouted while running. "Is that all you got? You all suck!"

His plan was working. The cuddlebears were becoming enraged as they repeatedly tried to steal the ball away from Macho, and he evaded them. He began sticking his tongue out at them.

Macho yelled, "Come on, you sissies! Catch me if you can!"

All the cuddlebears were completely consumed with rage. TooCool yelled out, "Impale that mofo!" and even the goalie began to chase Macho.

Macho continued to evade them. Macho was actually carefully maneuvering all the cuddlebears into the perfect position for his plan. The cuddlebears were so focused on hurting him that they didn't notice.

Finally, all the cuddlebears were positioned perfectly—they were all charging toward Macho in a

Machoponi

contracting circle—they were so furious that they were running full speed, with no concern about committing a foul. Macho stopped running, then calmly rolled his ball underneath his body. He stood still in the center of the contracting circle of hate. *It's so easy,* he thought.

Macho stuck out his tongue and waited.

Then at the right moment, Macho hopped up like Baryshnikov, while clasping the ball in his four legs. He shifted the ball in the air so that when he came back down, he landed on top of the ball, and he pushed down with his legs at the same time, causing a powerbounce just as the charging cuddlebears all shifted upright to impale Macho with their tummy quills. The ball with Macho on top bounced high up, and he was still in the air as the cuddlebears all crashed into each other in a group bellybump of pain, impaling and sticking to each other, erupting with blood.

And then Macho was coming back down with the ball beneath his hooves—the ball landed on a skewered cuddlebear's head, then bounced. Macho flung himself off, then crashed on his side into the ground, which hurt quite a bit. His ball bounced a short distance away, but it wasn't out of bounds.

After he got up, he stared at his ball. It had blotches of red on it—it was the second time he'd ever gotten blood on it.

"Please help us," said one of the cuddlebears

while spitting up blood.

"Why?" replied Macho. "It's not like I care."

Macho went to his ball, then went and scored an easy goal, since the goalie wasn't there. "Three to two. I win," he said.

90

Some of the cuddlebears were crying, others moaning. Some spat desperate-sounding insults. But they were no threat to Macho, because they were all stuck together in a big writhing mass, like a hairball of skewered bears.

Their blood pooled on the ground, staining the field.

Macho laughed at them, got his map, then started walking across the bridge.

Flutter-fly Poni Valley was next.

Flutter-fly Poni Valley

Macho walked for about three hours on the yellow brick road. As he did, he could feel the effects of the Cuddlebear Flare gradually wearing off, but not completely. He wasn't sure if he really cared about anything or not, and he wasn't sure it much mattered to him.

Off in the distance, he could see a hill, and as he approached it, he began to hear singing, but he couldn't quite make out the words. He decided he had to find out who was behind the hill. Maybe he should have been more cautious, but he really only cared a little.

He kicked his ball ahead of him, then galloped toward the hill and went around it.

Around the hill, he saw a group of about a dozen winged, gray ponies huddled around a trampoline in a field—the ponies' wings looked like gray moth wings, but otherwise they looked like regular undead ponies. They didn't seem to notice either him or his ball which

had come to rest a short distance away.

A female winged poni was boinging up and down on the trampoline and was singing:

I believe I can try!
I believe I can bounce real high!
Take my wings and spread them wide!
For a little bit, pretend to glide!

92

Then the trampolining poni saw Machoponi and diminished her bouncing until she was standing. She looked at Macho and said, "Who are you?"

"My name is Machoponi, Macho for short," Macho replied, as the group of winged ponies turned to look at him.

The winged poni hopped off the trampoline, then said, "I'm Superfly."

"It's nice to meet you, Superfly."

Superfly looked Machoponi up and down, then said, "You're strangely colored. You seem to be a mix of purple and gray!"

In alarm, Macho looked down at his front legs. It was true! His legs were gray with blotches of purple. The purple seemed to be fading from his normal color, and he was turning gray. Macho figured he should lie again, so he said, "Well, yes, err, I was playing dodgeball with some blokes and they had painted part of the balls

Machoponi

with purple paint, and well, I guess I'm not the greatest dodgeball player." Some of the winged ponies laughed, but Superfly stood with a stern expression on her face.

Superfly looked over at Macho's blue ball, which still had some blotches of dried blood on it. "Is that one of the balls you used?"

"Yes," Macho said, hoping it was the right thing to say.

"Well, the blotches on it don't look purple. They look dark red."

"Well, errr, yes. This one hit one of my opponents in the face. The sissy quit right after that. He couldn't bear it anymore."

Superfly shrugged.

Macho was suddenly struck by the idea that the winged ponies might be able to quickly fly him to the rope bridge. He decided to ask them. "I was wondering if there was some way you could possibly fly me to the Princess's castle."

Superfly and the other winged ponies glared at him.

Macho stammered, "If you'd like I can pay you with this map I have. I know it's not much, but it's very important for me to get to the rope bridge in front of the Princess's castle quickly."

Superfly screamed in rage, "How dare you!"

Macho took a step back, overwhelmed with

93

confusion. "Wh—what?"

Superfly seemed to relax as she watched Macho. "Don't you know?" she said. "How could you not know?"

"I'm sorry. I don't know what you're talking about."

Superfly stared at the ground. "We can't fly. None of us flutter-fly ponies can. Our wings don't work."

Suddenly, Macho understood why they had been using the trampoline. "I'm sorry. I didn't know."

94

Superfly seemed to be watching him for any sign of deceit. "Okay," she finally said. "So we can't fly you to the rope bridge. Even if we wanted to, which we don't."

Just then, Macho's tummy grumbled.

Superfly sneered, then said, "You sound hungry. Would you like some food?"

"Why yes, I'd be very grateful for some."

"Oh, you would, would you?"

"Yes."

"Ha, well, too bad, because you can't have any of ours, moron!"

Macho pouted. "Well, I guess I'll be moving on then, but if I may be so bold, may I ask exactly why you cannot fly? I can see that you all have wings...."

Superfly scowled. "Well, before, in the days of yore, before the Dark Kingdom became dark, the flutter-fly ponies could all fly and we all had the colorful wings

96

of butterflies. But after the Great Dividing, the flutter-fly ponies all became gray, not pastel like we used to be, and our wings became the wings of moths."

"And that's why you can't fly?" Macho blurted.

"You're interrupting."

"Sorry."

"No, the flutter-fly ponies could still fly, but one day, the Princess came down and watched the flutter-fly ponies flying, and, well, she grew extremely jealous, you see, because she couldn't fly at all, not even a little bit. Oh, she could hop and jump off things to be in the air for a while, but no, she couldn't fly. And so she put a curse on the flutter-fly ponies, and from that day forward, the flutter-fly ponies could no longer fly." Superfly gave Macho a sad, sad expression.

And Macho couldn't help but feel compassion for poor Superfly and all her fellow ponies. He cared so much, actually, that he figured that the Cuddlebear Flare had finally worn off on him.

Macho still had questions, so he asked, "Is that why you use the trampoline? Where did it come from?"

"The trampoline is a relic from the Time When People Walked with Ponies. We each take our turns on it. How sad we are—we bounce up and down and we spread our wings and pretend. But we always come back down." She pouted. A single tear even rolled from her eye, and down her face.

Machoponi

Macho felt a wave of sadness come over him at hearing the flutter-fly ponies' plight. He was consumed by the desire to *help*. "I heard the song you sang. Do you all sing that song when you bounce on the trampoline?"

"Yes," said Superfly. "It is a song we sing to comfort ourselves, because even though we know we will never be able to fly, at least we can pretend, for a little bit. And pretending is fun." She broke into sobs.

And at that moment, Macho was struck by an idea. Perhaps it was because he had grown up in a pastel world, surrounded by positive thinking, or perhaps it was because he himself believed so strongly in the power of belief—but whatever the case was, he found himself asking a simple question: "Have you ever believed you can *fly*? From what I heard, you only believe you can *try*. But trying is not doing. There is no try or try not. There is only do or do not."

Superfly rolled her teary eyes. "Yeah, right, what's the point of trying if you're only destined to fail? You only get hurt that way."

"Please, you've got to believe! Anything is possible...if you believe."

She shook her head. "I dunno...."

"You've got to believe! Just believe! Even if you have no reason to, even if everything you know tells you that you won't succeed! You've got to believe!"

"I...dunno."

97

Lotus Rose

Now Macho was screaming, "Beeeeliiieeeeveeee!!! Get on the trampoline and believe!!"

"I believe!"

"Bounce and believe! Don't just believe you can *try.* Believe you can *fly!*"

98

Superfly started hopping, building up her momentum while half-yelling, half-singing, "I belliiieeevee I can flyyyyyyy!!!!"

Each bounce became bouncier as she stayed up longer—she spread her wings and flapped, then on the sixth bounce, a wonderific, fantabulous thing happened! She didn't come back down at all!

She was flying!

Macho shouted up at her, "See! That's what happens...when you believe!"

Superfly swooped and soared while laughing maniacally.

The other winged ponies watched her, then they began to spread their wings and flap them and lift off the ground as they sang a song:

They each sang:

I believe I can fly.
I believe that there is no try.
There is only do or don't do it.
If you just try, then it's bullpucky.

Machoponi

Macho watched and felt his eyes moisten at seeing such a beautiful spectacle. The winged ponies began flying in trails like birds in the sky, and Macho's jaw dropped. He watched them for a while before deciding to ask them something. He yelled up at Superfly, "Now that I helped you fly, do you think you can give me a lift?"

Superfly laughed mockingly and the others joined in. She hovered in front of Macho, then said, "Awwww hell no, four-limbs! We aren't gonna do anything for you if you're too dumb to fly."

"But I helped you!" Macho shouted in outrage.

"You didn't help us. It was because we believed in ourselves that we learned to fly."

"But I helped you believe in yourself!"

"Whatever, four-limbs."

"Why do you keep calling me four-limbs?"

"Because," replied Superfly, "you only have four legs and no wings, so you suck. We, however have *six* limbs."

Macho shouted angrily, "Yeah, like a spider!"

"No, spiders have eight limbs, dum-dum."

Then all the ponies started singing again, and this is what they sang:

We believe we are more
Better than you guys with limbs of four.
Don't need to bounce on no trampoline.
Just fly above and be real mean.

100

They stopped singing, then Superfly said, "Why don't you go away and take that stupid trampoline with you? You can use it to go over the wall on the edge of the Chill-Aid Man's Territory."

"Would that work?"

"Well, you won't be able to cross the wall by yourself. But maybe, just maybe, if you bounce high enough on the trampoline you can get over. You could go to a tunnel to the east, but the chocolate bunnies would definitely kill you."

"What about the Chill-Aid Man?"

"Oh, he'll try to kill you too, but he's not as bad as the bunnies."

"Great," muttered Machoponi. "Can you tell me anything else about the Chill-Aid Man?"

"Yeah, he's a dork—and tell him not to be so bloody positive all the time. This is the Dark Kingdom after all. Now, the trampoline has wheels that come out and a motor to drive it. It doesn't go fast, but it goes. Just take it out of here. And take yourself with it, dorkhead. I'm done talking to you."

Humiliated, Macho prepared to drive the trampoline.

The Territory of the Chill-Aid Man was next.

The Territory of the Chill-Aid Man

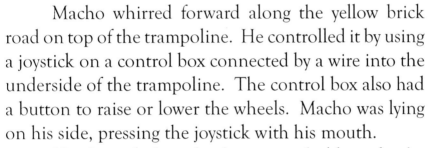

Macho whirred forward along the yellow brick road on top of the trampoline. He controlled it by using a joystick on a control box connected by a wire into the underside of the trampoline. The control box also had a button to raise or lower the wheels. Macho was lying on his side, pressing the joystick with his mouth.

He figured that the humans who'd made the trampoline meant for the wheels to be used just to make the trampoline easier to move, and not as a mode of transportation, because it didn't move very fast, and the wheels were small. Macho was driving forward at the rate of a fast walk.

It was absolutely amazing to Macho what the humans had created during the time they had existed. They had been able to create things, such as the rope bridge, that no poni could ever create. It was said that the humans used to have things called hands and thumbs which allowed them to move things around much easier than a poni could. And the ponies now

marveled at the ancient relics left behind.

After about two hours of driving, he saw the wall in the distance. The wall went to the left and right as far as the eye could see, and Macho could see no tunnels.

In front of the wall, to the left of the road, he could make out a red blob.

Macho figured it was highly likely that the blob was the Chill-Aid Man. And indeed, as he got closer, the red figure stood up, rising on red legs. Macho could make out the figure now: it looked like a giant clear pitcher filled with a red liquid. It had two red arms and two red legs, and a happy face that looked like it was drawn on the side of the pitcher.

Macho drove onward. He had to keep on the road, because the small trampoline wheels wouldn't have worked on the grass.

He was almost there. The road went all the way up to the wall. The wall, he could now see, was comprised of bricks and was several ponies high—definitely too high for a poni to go over without trampolining.

The pitcher stood watching as Macho and his traveling trampoline approached. The pitcher appeared to be about two ponies high—it was very still and seemed in good humor—at least he kept smiling the whole time. He didn't blink, which Macho thought was kind of eery.

Macho stopped the trampoline in front of the

Machoponi

wall. He stood up on the trampoline and called out, "Hello! Are you the Chill-Aid Man?"

The pitcher waved and then, in a creepy, raspy deep voice, replied, "Oh yeahhhhhh!"

Macho was taken aback but tried to hide it. He hopped onto the ground. "Well, it's nice to meet you. I'm Macho, short for Machoponi."

"Nice to meet you too, oh yeahhhh!"

"Are you going to kill me?"

"Probably. It's what I've done with all the other ponies who came through here, well at least ever since after the Dark Kingdom became dark. But first, I'd like to have a conversation. We can each tell our story! Shall I go first, or shall you? That's always the hardest part—deciding who goes first and who goes second in things."

Macho thought that maybe if he went first, the Chill-Aid Man might simply kill him right afterward, so he said, "Why don't you go first? So, wow. You've been around since the time of the Great Dividing?"

The Chill-Aid Man frantically shook his arms around. "Oh yeahhhhhh! And I used to be so much happier when things were pastel."

"How come?"

"Well, in the days of yore, I used to be filled with punch and there were human children who, when they became thirsty, I would punch through a wall and pour

103

them punch from my very own head. And I would shout out, 'oh yeahhhh.' It was like my catchphrase. But there are no more humans, except for the Princess, and when the Dark Kingdom became dark, the punch inside me transformed into blood. And one day, the Princess put a spell on me, so that I can no longer punch through walls! I've tried. And besides, there are no more thirsty children around anymore. I think I was happier when I was filled with punch."

Then he began sadly singing this song:

I Used to Have Punch

Oh, I used to have punch!
And I used to get drunk
By little kids.
And nothing is better than kids giggling with glee,
While drinking the red punch right out of me!

Oh, I used to have punch!
And I burst through a bunch
Of flimsy walls.
And nothing is better than giving kids punch,
And getting so drunk by the whole happy bunch!

Macho nodded and said, "That sucks."

"What does?"

"That there are no more children to serve."

"It kinda does. But I do enjoy killing, too," he said with a smile.

"It has its appeal." And Macho meant it. He'd never killed anyone before coming to the Dark Kingdom. But he'd kinda killed the cuddlebears—or he'd at least badly maimed them—and being murderous was growing on him. Maybe it had something to do with his coat turning gray. He asked the Chill-Aid Man, "But why not serve the undead ponies with your blood? They'd enjoy drinking blood."

105

"Well, I dunno. I became used to children. Ponies are strange to me. Besides, ever since the Dark Kingdom became dark, I've been filled with consuming murderous hate."

"Ah, I see. Are you still gonna kill me?"

"Yeah. I'm gonna churn up your bones and add your blood to the other ponies' blood inside of me." The smile never left his face.

Macho nodded forlornly, then thought for a moment. "So what ever happened to the humans?"

The limbed pitcher shrugged. "I really don't know. One day, they just disappeared. The Princess is the only one I know of that's left. If I could only get past this wall, I could go talk to her and maybe convince her to remove her curse—maybe serve her a drink of

poni blood. Maybe she's thirsty. Oh yeahhhh." His voice sounded sad, but the smile never left his face.

Macho realized that he hadn't known the Princess was human until just a few minutes ago. There was so much he was learning about the Dark Kingdom. He wanted to ask many more questions, but he was in a hurry, so instead he asked, "Why can't you get past the wall? Aren't there tunnels to the west and east?"

"I'm too big," the Chill-Aid man said sadly while smiling.

"Hmmm. Could you maybe go around the wall? My map shows that you can go around it if you go far enough."

"I'm scared. There are creatures even more dangerous than me to the east and west—chocolate bunnies and jumbo shrimps!"

"Oh my!" Macho exclaimed, then he thought some more, swishing his mouth from side to side. "Tell me more about this curse the Princess put on you."

"Well, one day she came to see me. She drank some blood and seemed real sweet until I showed her how I could punch through walls, so she got furious and put a curse on me. I think she was jealous. Then she left. I think she left to visit the flying ponies."

"Hmmmm. A curse? She put a curse on the flutter-fly ponies too."

"Yes, I tried and tried to punch through the wall,

but I couldn't."

"Oh, that sucks."

"It most certainly does suck a lot! Oh, but that's enough about me. I'd like to hear your story now."

"Well, um, you mean what's happened to me recently?"

"Yeah, recent is better. What have you been up to lately?"

So Macho quickly told the Chill-Aid Man about his adventures with the cuddlebears and the flutter-fly ponies.

"Ooh, what a great story!" exclaimed the Chill-Aid Man. "Do you have a song about your recent adventures?"

"Um, well, I can make one up."

The Chill-Aid Man almost squealed in delight! "Oooh yeahhh, I love songs! If a person sings a good enough song, I spare their life!"

So with a quivery voice, Macho began to sing this song (his voice grew steadier as he went on):

Now listen up!
Because cuddles are pain!
They wanna play with your ball,
And it'll drive you insane!
You want someone to hold,
Because you feel so cold.

107

Machoponi

But their touch grows sharp!
It keeps you far apart!
Ohhhhh....
They've got the cuds that kill!
They've got the cuds that kill!

Now here come more pricks,
Because there're ponies that fly,
And they will put you down,
And their opinion is high!
And they're real real cruel!
Give you a trampolee-een.
Treat you like a fool,
Cuz they're so so mean!

Ohhhhh....
They've got the wings that thrill!
They've got the wings that thrill!

109

Chill-Aid Man tried to clap but his arms were too far apart and too short. "Best song ever!" he exclaimed. "You just *have* to make a third verse about me! Sing it to me when you're done!"

"Thank you," Macho said, then bowed. "So you aren't gonna kill me?"

"Oh, I'm still gonna kill you."

"But you said if you liked my song you would

spare my life."

"No I didn't."

"Did too."

"No, I said, if a person sings a good enough song, I spare their life! And *you* aren't a person!" Then the Chill-Aid Man started chuckling. "I can't believe you fell for that! You think you're people!"

Macho pouted and thought desperately.

110

The Chill-Aid Man stared at him for a while before muttering, "Guess I'll kill you now."

"Wait! How can I come up with a third verse if you kill me?"

"Oh yeah. Well, nevermind that then. I'm gonna pulverize your body and let your red juice fill me!"

Finally Macho came up with an idea! "Wait! What if I figured out a way that you could punch through the wall?"

"Oh yeahhhh! I would be so grateful! Then I could go visit the Princess!"

"Cool! I'm headed in the same direction! We could help each other and travel together as companions in a great adventure!"

"Well I don't see how we can do that after I kill you."

"So don't kill me! It would be my reward for helping you."

"Oh nahhhh, I'm still gonna kill you, then I'll

break through the wall. So what's this idea you've come up with for me to do it?"

Macho blinked twice. "Nevermind. I was thinking about a way to punch through *whales*."

"Oh," said the Chill-Aid Man in a disappointed voice. "Guess I'll tear you limb from limb and drain the glorious red gore out of your flaccid body now."

"Wait!" Macho shouted. "I have another idea!"

"Yes?" said the Chill-Aid Man hopefully.

"You can use the trampoline to go over the wall! That's why I brought it here, because I was gonna bounce on it to go over the wall myself."

111

"Hey, that's a great idea! Thank you. Should I kill you now?"

In a scolding tone, Macho said, "No no no. First we have to decide who goes first and who goes second."

"Oh yeah, that's always the hardest thing to decide isn't it?"

Macho didn't say a word and pretended to think hard. "Oh, I know! I'll go first!"

The Chill-Aid Man just looked at him with that creepy grin on his face. Then he shook his head and the blood inside him sloshed. "Ohhh, nahhhhh! I'm not gonna fall for *that*. Because if *you* go first, you will just run away before I get the chance to hop over the wall. There is only one alternative, and that is that *I* go

first. See, that way, when you go over the wall, I'll be waiting for you and I can kill you."

Macho nodded solemnly. "It's all very logical. I guess you've figured it out."

"Yes, well, I do have some common sense. I'm not an air head, if you know what I mean." It seems like he would have winked, but his expression remained frozen in a smile.

112

"Do you need some encouragement with your trampolining?" Macho asked as the Chill-Aid Man crawled up the trampoline.

"Why would you want to help me when you're about to be killed by me?" the Chill-Aid Man asked, sounding genuinely confused.

"Well, I don't hold grudges. I know you're just doing what a formerly-punch-filled-plastic-head-who's-now-filled-with-blood does."

The Chill-Aid Man nodded on top of the trampoline and the blood inside him sloshed. He kicked the blue ball off the trampoline onto the ground, then said, "So encourage, then." He took a timid hop that was slightly amplified by the elastic material of the trampoline. The blood inside his head slightly-sloshed.

Macho threw all his effort into encouragement, shouting, "Bouncy bouncy! You can bounce if you want to! You can leave the ground behind!"

Machoponi

The Chill-Aid Man began bouncing a little more boldly, the elasticizing quality of the trampoline doing its amplifying.

Macho yelled out, "Are you with me?!?!? Bouncy bouncy!!!!!"

And the Chill-Aid Man started to take to it, yelling back, "Bouncy bouncy!" as his round, plastic body-head began to rise more and more and more sloshing took place.

"Higher higher!" Macho yelled. "More bouncy bouncy!"

And the Chill-Aid Man complied, and the liquid inside him was sloshing up and down the inside edges of his container-body, but he was so excited, because he was almost high enough for his feet to reach the top of the wall.

"Bounce to this!" shouted Macho. "Bounce like you've never bounced before! Superbounce! Do it!"

And as the Chill-Aid Man descended to contact feet with trampoline, he deep-knee-bended and superbounced, while shouting, "Oh yeahhhhh!!!!"

And a gush of red flung out the top of his head, which was not only his head, but his whole body. It went beyond its container and spilled and splattered all around as the Chill-Aid Man grinned and screamed in terror.

He was only half full as he landed. He no longer

seemed enthusiastic about bouncing and seemed to be trying to stop it.

He was wobbly, but somehow, barely, managed to keep his balance as he bounced a few more times. He was no doubt thinking that he might survive if he could just decelerate and get off the trampoline.

114

But, "BOUNCY BOUNCY!!" shouted Macho as he initiated a super-move, as he flipped his ball into the air with his hind legs. As the ball descended, he kicked it hard with his hind legs. And the ball flew right into the Chill-Aid Man's unending grin—and the Chill-Aid Man toppled over, his balance completely gone now as he tipped off the edge of the trampoline with much spillage.

Macho's ball came to rest about forty feet away, and it was drenched in red. It was the third time he'd gotten blood on his ball.

The Chill-Aid Man was lying on his side on the red-drenched grass, unmoving and mostly empty.

Macho nudged him with his hoof and the Chill-Aid Man tottered a little and continued smiling. His arms and legs were limp. He seemed quite broken.

Macho stared at him for a little bit, then he began to sing:

Oh, he bounced right up!
Went way too high!

Machoponi

Oversized plastic head.
What a goofy guy!
He's got a perma-grin,
And a lust for red.
Gonna drain the gore in,
And then you'll be real dead!

But he's got the blood that spills!
That spillllls!
He's got the blood that spills!

115

Bouncing
for Love

116

Macho knelt and slipped his head inside the pitcher that lay on its side on the grass. He lapped at the small amount of blood that was still inside. His legs trembled as he did so, because it was now painfully clear that he was one of the undead.

But it lessened his hunger.

With a sickly feeling, he kicked his blue ball up and watched it go over the

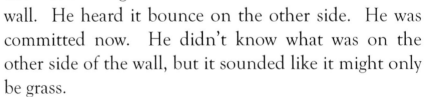

wall. He heard it bounce on the other side. He was committed now. He didn't know what was on the other side of the wall, but it sounded like it might only be grass.

He hopped onto the trampoline. Then he took a deep breath and began to bounce.

Bounce.

He bounced because he wanted to look into her eyes again. There had always been a sadness to her, as if the world had always been too much for her. Her pendant of half a broken heart had always been a fitting piece of jewelry.

Bounce!

He bounced for her mischievous, beautiful eyes and her sweet voice. And also for her scar—she was a flawed beauty, with her scar as a symbol of the ugliness that hides beneath pastel exteriors.

Bounce!!

For her love of potpies and dancing. And all the parts of their lives they had shared together—having fun and growing up and dealing with peers and crappy parents—and the time she'd told him her father had bitten her one day in a drunken rage—she'd told Macho he could never reveal the secret—and the bite had become her scar.

BOUNCE!!!

For all her rebukes and cruelty, which only kept his yearning alive for all these years. He had been chasing her ever since they were little, and here he was chasing her again. And even though he didn't know how he would ever be able to bring her back to the pastel side, he had to do this, because he loved her.

For a moment, he feared he might not to be able to make it, but he gritted his teeth and strained, putting

all he could into one final, massive superbounce and he just barely cleared the wall and went over.

He landed on the grassy ground on the other side then dropped and rolled. He felt pain in his right front leg and the right side of his body, but he didn't think he was injured. He stood up and looked around, and as he stared at the rope bridge about thirty feet away with the goat standing in front of it, he couldn't stop thinking about Dust. He was remembering one night when he and Dust were twelve years old and they had stolen a potpie off of a windowsill. They'd shared it together and that night they'd kissed. It had been Macho's first kiss. And they didn't get caught.

118

Praise the Infurnal Goat

Machoponi retrieved his ball then began walking toward the bridge. He could see a gray, horned, four-legged goat standing in front of it. The bridge was made up of wooden planks connected to ropes which held the bridge up. The ropes were tied to stakes driven into the ground on each side of the chasm. The yellow brick road went from the wall to the bridge, then continued on the other side of a chasm to a gray castle a short distance away.

Macho walked closer. The goat was wearing a black sweater with a turtleneck. He had a scraggly dirty silver beard. And there was something strange on his forehead—some kind of symbol.

As Macho walked up, the goat shouted, "Hail!"

Macho looked up into the sky, but there was no rain or hail or anything.

"No no," said the goat. "I meant 'hello.'"

"Oh, um, hey, how's it going? I'm Machoponi, Macho for short."

"Dark greetings! It's nice to infurnally meet you, fellow undead abomination! I am known as... Billphomet!"

"Billphomet? Nice to meet you. What does 'infurnally' mean?"

The goat rolled his eyes, then answered, "It means I'm in fur. I'm wearing a cashmere sweater!"

"Ohhhh," Macho said while nodding. "And what does 'abomination' mean?"

"Ummmmm...I'm not quite sure. I think it means 'undead.'"

"Ohhhh, well why not just say 'undead'?"

The goat rolled his eyes. "Well it just doesn't sound as cool, does it?"

Macho thought about it for a moment, then agreed. He found himself staring at the black symbol on the goat's forehead. It was a broken heart inside a circle with two horns on top.

"So," said the goat. "Do you want to cross the bridge?"

"I'm not sure."

"Well, if you want to cross, you must answer my riddle."

"So if I get it wrong, you will kill me?"

"Oh, nahhh, I wouldn't do that. I just want you to answer, that's all. It doesn't even have to be the *right* answer. Come on, you'll like my riddle. Wanna hear it?"

120

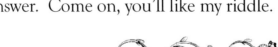

Machoponi

"Well, I'm not sure if I want to cross the bridge yet."

Billphomet pouted.

Macho continued, "I need to find out if you've seen a female poni come through here today. She has a tramp stamp and is named Dust. Did she come through?"

Billphomet shook his head. "Nobody has been through here for over a week."

"You're sure?"

"Oh, absolutely! It is my duty to guard the bridge for my dark mistress. No one comes through here without me knowing about it."

"Oh, okay. Well I guess I'll just wait here until she gets here."

Billphomet pouted again, then asked, "Don't you want to hear my riddle?"

"But I don't need to cross, so I don't need to hear it."

Billphomet looked like he was about to cry. "Oh come on! You'll like it. Don't be a spoilsport!"

"Well, can I think about the answer, then answer later? If I'm gonna answer a riddle, I want to try to get it right."

Billphomet grinned. "Of course! Are you ready?"

Macho nodded.

"Okay," said Billphomet. "Harken to my riddle:

what grows colder as it melts?"

Macho thought for a few minutes while Billphomet watched his face, but Macho couldn't think of the answer. Finally, Macho said, "I'll have to think about it."

"It's a pretty cool riddle isn't it? I made it up myself."

To be polite, Macho answered, "Yes, very cool."

"Do you praise me?"

"Um, sure."

"I have a song, too. A very evil song. Do you want to hear it?"

"Um, sure."

Very evil guitars started to play along with blastbeat drumming. Billphomet put on a scowl, then started grunting deathmetal style vocals, and the voice actually reminded Macho a lot of the Chill-Aid Man. Macho couldn't understand a single word the goat grunted, but he did notice that Billphomet bleated evilly near the end of it.

When the song was over, Macho said, "I couldn't understand a single word you said."

Billphomet rolled his eyes. "Well you're not really supposed to, but I can tell you the lyrics of the song called:

Lotus Rose

Praise the Infurnal Goat

Praise the dark princess, corrupt and golden-haired,
Who brought us the dark when she no longer cared.
I wear her mark upon my head,
And voice my greetings to the dead.

Praise the infurnal goat, who is me.
Embrace necrofeelya and blasphemy!
Bring down the Kingdom of Pastel,
And burn it in the fires of hellllllll!!!!!

124

BAAAAAAAHH!!!!!!

Nod your head and praise the goat,
Undead warriors of the night.
Topple the Kingdom of Pastel.

Macho felt the evil of the lyrics seeping into him and he found them oddly compelling. Self-consciously he looked down at his legs. There was no more pastel left—it was all gray.

Macho looked at Billphomet then said, "Those are some sick lyrics. But I have a question though. What does 'necrofeelya' mean?"

"Oh, that's when the undead cuddle."

Machoponi

Macho nodded. "Oh. And what does 'blasphemy' mean?"

"It's when you use curse words."

"Like 'mofo?'"

"No, like, cunt, slut, pussy, bastard, and shit."

"Oh. I don't know what any of those words mean."

Billphomet nodded.

"So..." Macho said, "What does 'cunt' mean?"

But just then, out of the corner of his eye, he saw something.

On the horizon, four gray four-legged figures were walking.

125

Reunited

126

Macho watched the approaching figures without saying a word. They were coming from the opposite direction Macho had come from, so they had obviously chosen a different route. As they got closer, he recognized Dust—her tail and mane had turned dirty silver and the rest of her was gray. Next to her was Darkeyes with his horned hairstyle. There were also two other male undead ponies who he didn't recognize.

Dust smiled at him briefly and Darkeyes scowled the whole time. Macho noticed that Darkeyes was wearing a saddle.

Billphomet stood in front of the bridge behind Macho, as Macho walked up to meet the undead ponies. Darkeyes snarled, then said, "What the hell are you doing here?"

"I came to bring Dust back."

Darkeyes laughed. "How do you propose to do that? She's undead now."

Macho looked at Dust, and noticed her eyes now looked like cat's eyes. He replied, "I...don't know how I'll do it, but I'll find a way. You've kidnapped her and

I'm going to free her. I'll fight you if I have to."

Darkeyes chuckled, then said, "We haven't kidnapped her. She came voluntarily, didn't you, Dust?"

"Yes," answered Dust. "You shouldn't have come here, Macho, but I'm so flattered you did. You cared about me so much that you became undead to find me?"

"Yes," answered Macho. "Well, I died of a broken heart. I don't just care about you, Dust. I love you."

"Wow," Dust said. "You really must. I love you too."

Macho found himself grinning uncontrollably.

Dust grinned back—she had the sharp incisors of the undead. "But," she said, "I have to go to the castle and meet with the Princess. It's part of the deal we made."

"What are you talking about, Dust? What deal?"

Dust giggled, then said, "I'll tell you, but first you gotta check out the change I made to my tramp stamp. Check it out." She presented her side to Macho.

Now he could see that the tramp stamp symbol now had two horns drawn on top. It was identical to the symbol on Billphomet's forehead: a broken heart inside a circle with two horns.

He gasped. "Dust, what are you doing? You did that on purpose?"

"Of course, I'm one of the undead now. The symbol is called the corruptagram. I came to the dark side on purpose. It was part of the deal."

"What deal?"

"Clint made a deal with Darkeyes. They traded me for a bunch of shipments of chocolate mints to be smuggled over the Jagged Line."

Darkeyes laughed, then said, "So Clint got Dust to cross over in order to meet the Princess, but I'm glad to say I screwed Clint over. He didn't get any more chocolate mints from me! Did you know he made me act like I was scared of him that one time he crossed the line? So he got what he deserved."

Macho suddenly understood Clint's behavior. "So the only reason Clint helped me chase you was so he could get revenge?"

"It seems that way," Darkeyes said.

Macho started to plead with Dust, "Please, let me take you back! We'll find a way! Anything is possible if you believe! Come back to the pastel side! Please, I love you, Dust!"

Dust shook her head, then said, "I wish I could, but I can't. I have to bring my half of the broken heart pendant to the Princess. She has the other half. It's my destiny, Macho. It's what I was born for."

"Please Dust," Macho pleaded, "you don't have to do anything! They didn't even fulfill their half of the

bargain! I love you, don't you see? Come with me. I never want to be apart from you!"

"You say you love me, but after a day or so in the Dark Kingdom, you will be completely transformed and you won't care anymore. They don't have love here. But maybe we can hang out. We can just spend our days having fun and eating chocolate mints! You just have to wait a little bit."

"I don't ever want to stop loving you!" Tears streamed down Macho's face. The other undead ponies rolled their eyes. "I won't let you go across that bridge! Soon it will be too late, and I can't let that happen! I'll find a way! And if our love will only last a day, I want to be with you the whole time."

Dust glanced at Darkeyes, who nodded, then she said, "Okay, I'll stay for a day. Darkeyes and the others can wait for me. We can share our last moments of love together, and it'll be enhanced by the chocolate mints." Dust went to the saddle on Darkeye's back and opened a pocket. She brought out a piece of chocolate candy, then chewed it and swallowed it. She brought another piece of candy out with her mouth and held it out to Macho, who grabbed it in his mouth but didn't chew it.

Dust said, "Please eat it, Macho. You remember when you had mints before, right? Remember how pleasurable they were? If you love me, you'll eat it. It'll

make our love even stronger."

Macho flipped the candy into his mouth, then began to chew. He felt a swoosh of cold throughout his mouth as the candy began to melt, then he swallowed it. He was suddenly reminded of the cold feeling in his mouth he'd felt after kissing Badunkadunk and Dust at the promenade. He wondered if he'd been set up back then. Had Dust intoxicated him on purpose?

130

He felt a wave of euphoria and started grinning dopily. He was finding it difficult to continue his line of thought.

He stared at Dust and she smiled at him. She walked up to him and kissed him and Macho couldn't help but kiss her back, knowing that it was perhaps the last time, and their tongues mingled and Macho felt the cold sensation again. Then he was dizzy and fell to the ground.

He lay with his face on the side of the ground, watching Dust and the other undead ponies walking away. He tried to rise to his feet but could only partially get up. And he watched in dismay as Dust talked with Billphomet. It looked like the goat was posing his riddle to her. Dust answered. Billphomet nodded, then stood aside to let the ponies cross the bridge.

And Macho called out to her, but she never turned around as they crossed the bridge, walked to the castle, and as the drawbridge lowered and they went inside.

Machoponi

After a few minutes, Macho was able to stand again. He staggered over to Billphomet, who said, "If you want to cross, you must answer my riddle."

"Okay," Macho said.

"What grows colder as it melts?"

"A chocolate mint."

"Ah, very good. You have to be careful with those things you know. You don't have as high a tolerance as that girl Dust seems to have."

Macho nodded sadly. "I've got to catch up with them. Do you know where they went?"

"Yeah, they went to visit the Princess. Is she expecting you too?"

"No."

"Well, you can talk to the guards, and if the Princess is in a good mood, she'll see you."

"Okay, thank you," Macho said as he stepped onto the bridge. Then, out of curiosity, he turned around and asked, "Did Dust answer your riddle?"

"Yes, she did, but she gave a different answer from you. I'm not sure it really fit, but it was original. I liked it."

"What was her answer?"

"She said: 'A girl's heart.'"

The Princess

132

Macho walked unsteadily across the bridge, then up to the drawbridge of the castle. A guard poni on the top of the wall called down to him, "Are you Machoponi?"

Macho answered that he was.

The guard shouted, "The Princess wishes to see you! She said to tell you that Dust is with her." The drawbridge was then lowered.

The guards inside the castle escorted Macho through the halls. He still felt quite intoxicated as he walked down the hallways, then into the throne room. On the far end of the large room, he could see Dust with her back turned to him. He didn't see Darkeyes and the two other male undead ponies. Dust was standing in front of a very thin, blonde sixteen-year-old human girl who was sitting on a throne and blowing bubbles by dipping a wand into a bottle, then blowing through a circle in the wand. Macho had never seen a human being before, other than in books. One of the guards

Machoponi

whispered into Macho's ear, "That girl is the Princess."

"Hello Machoponi!" the girl called out. "Come closer!"

The guards departed and Macho began walking forward. The sound of his hooves echoed off the marble floor.

Dust turned around and smiled as he approached.

133

The Princess wore a black corset with purple fringe and a long black dress—she had a tiara on her head and black lace gloves on her hands. Her eyes were heavily lined and she also wore black nail polish. Around her neck hung a pendant that looked nearly identical to Dust's—it was a ruby in the shape of half a heart—a jagged line was on its left side, as if the other half of the heart had been torn away.

Macho stopped next to Dust, then bowed to the Princess. Bubbles floated and wobbled through the air.

They would pop against him every once in a while.

The Princess put the bubble wand into the bottle, closed it, then set it on the inside edge of her throne. Macho could now clearly see how thin the Princess was. Her cheeks were sunken. She looked sick. But maybe it was okay for humans to look like that, he thought.

134

"I'm so glad to meet you," said the Princess. "Dust has told me a little bit about you in the short time we've talked. I'm impressed by your dedication to her."

Dust looked over at him and smiled, and Macho found he was suddenly unable to keep from blushing.

"Th-thank you," he said.

"You're welcome. So what do you think of the Dark Kingdom?"

Macho didn't want to risk offending the Princess, so he said, "It's very nice."

The Princess rolled her eyes. "Oh, please. What do you really think?"

"Well, it's been a little dangerous for me, but I've only seen a small part."

The Princess nodded. "Well, I control all its parts. I'm the Princess. You may call me, Megan, though."

"Okay, Megan."

"I bet you've never seen a human before. I'm the last one left. Can I ask you a question? Do I look fat to you? Everyone around here is scared to tell me the truth."

"No, not at all."

The Princess huffed. "You're lying. I've put on a pound lately, but I haven't eaten for three days now, so I should be okay soon."

Macho simply nodded, scared to say the wrong thing.

The Princess looked at Dust and asked, "Do I look fat to you?"

"Just a little," said Dust.

"See that wasn't so hard. But anyway," said the Princess as she looked back down at Macho. "Dust told me about you, and I truly am impressed. I think it's so beautiful that you would try to rescue the one you love like that. You have love. All that love has ever done to *me* is hurt me. So I made it go away."

"I don't understand," said Macho. "What do you mean?"

"Well, I'm the reason there is a Dark Kingdom and why there are no more people anymore, don't you know that?"

Macho shook his head.

The Princess scowled. "I guess you ponies over there in the pastel side don't know much about me."

Macho shook his head timidly.

"Well, you see there was a time long ago, way before you were born, when humans hung out with the ponies. I was alive way back then. But I got so sick of

135

people. They really weren't all that wonderful. So, one day, on my sixteenth birthday, they made me Princess for a Day, so I decided that as Princess, my first order of business was to make all the people go away and to make a dark kingdom to suit my dark heart. And I still sit here today, wallowing in darkness. But you pastel ponies probably have no idea what that's like. You're so bright and cheery, you probably don't even understand what 'wallowing' means."

Before Macho could ask her what wallowing meant, the Princess began to sing her mournful song:

Princess for a Day

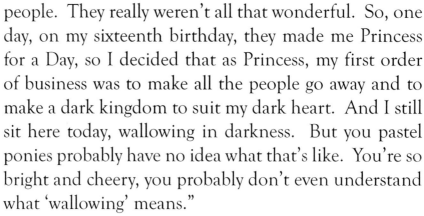

People told me to eat,
And each day to greet
All the others with a big smile.
Made me a princess,
For a day, a princess.
While I filled with the taste of my bile!

Go awayyyyy...I made them all go away.
Love, pastel, and people.
I made it all go away.
For a dayyyyy...made me Princess for a Day,
But they pissed me off too much,

Machoponi

So I made them all go away!

So, he loved me, he said,
'Til the day that he's dead,
But love was a poisonous flower!
Made me a princess,
For a day, a princess.
But they shouldn't have tempted my power.

Ohh, go away, I made it all go away!
They made me Princess. Princess for a day.
So I made them all go away!

"That's a touching song," Macho said when the Princess had finished.

Dust exclaimed, "That was beautiful!"

"Thank you," replied the Princess, then she almost smiled.

"You're welcome," said Macho. "Now, I hate to impose, but since you're the Princess and obviously have great power, is there any way you could help Dust and I get back to the Pastel Kingdom?"

The Princess thought for a moment. "Yes, I may be able to help, but you have to understand I can't just make things go however I want them to. Sometimes we are not as in control of things as we would like to be."

Macho nodded. "I can definitely relate."

138

The Princess said, "Do you know the whole reason I set up the trade of mints in exchange for meeting Dust?"

"No. You were behind it all?"

"Yes. I just had to see Dust, because well, you see, Dust is kind of like the poni version of me. Our destinies are connected. We're like soul-twins, and we each have one half of the amulet." She grabbed the jagged pendant around her neck and lifted it away from her chest.

Macho was struck speechless. He had no idea what to say or think. He looked at Dust, but Dust was speaking to the Princess.

Dust said to the Princess, "What are you talking about? This is crazy! Where did the amulet come from? Why did it get broken in half? What do you mean by soul-twins?"

The Princess answered Dust, "You're just the poni version of me—my 'poni-me.' Magic often does strange things. Like I've said, I don't really have a lot of control over things. All I know is that the amulet, when it was whole, was given to me by my former lover. But he ended up breaking my heart. One day, soon after the Dark Kingdom became dark, I broke the amulet in half on a rock. I kept one half and flung the other half across the Jagged Line—and since that day, love has been gone from the Dark Kingdom."

Machoponi

Dust gasped. "One of my ancestors claimed he saw a human girl throw my pendant across the Jagged Line into a pond. He recovered it, and since then, it's been passed down from generation to generation."

The Princess nodded, then replied, "But today, the other half of the amulet has returned to me! I think it's some kind of destiny thing."

Macho shouted angrily, "So destiny made everything come together just so Dust could bring you the half of the amulet? Is that what you're saying? Why couldn't you just get your precious amulet? Why did you have to bring Dust into it?"

"Yes," said the Princess. "I understand what you're saying. It doesn't seem fair. But only a sorrowful soul can keep the magic of the broken amulet alive. Dust was the only one who I could trust to carry the amulet half."

Macho almost felt like screaming out in rage, but controlled himself. And beside him, Dust was telling him, "Stay calm. Stay calm."

Macho shouted, "So what are you gonna do with this broken amulet, then? If she gives you the amulet, *then* can you help us get back to the Pastel Kingdom?"

The Princess suddenly seemed uncomfortable. "Let me explain about the amulet. When the two halves of the amulet are combined while a person or poni is wearing them, the two halves will combine, and

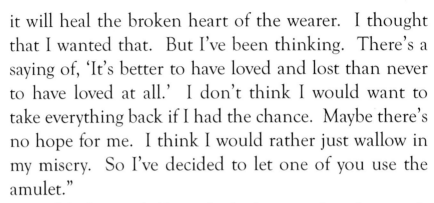

140

it will heal the broken heart of the wearer. I thought that I wanted that. But I've been thinking. There's a saying of, 'It's better to have loved and lost than never to have loved at all.' I don't think I would want to take everything back if I had the chance. Maybe there's no hope for me. I think I would rather just wallow in my misery. So I've decided to let one of you use the amulet."

Macho and Dust looked at each other with questioning expressions then looked back at the Princess. Then simultaneously, they asked her what she was talking about.

The Princess explained: "I believe that if someone died of a broken heart, then if they heal it with the amulet, it will bring them back to life. If the poni is standing next to the Jagged Line, they would then be able to cross back over. Dust told me you died of a broken heart, Macho."

Macho said, "Yes, but so did Dust."

The Princess nodded. "The amulet will only work on one poni, though. I'm sorry. You'll have to decide between yourselves."

With a stiff upper lip, Macho said, "Then it will be Dust, then. It's her amulet, anyway."

Dust looked over at him and in a choked up voice said, "You would do that for me?"

"Of course. I love you Dust."

Machoponi

Dust shook her head sadly. "You are a wonderful poni, Macho. You were always too good for me. Maybe you should go instead. You belong in the pastel side. It was like I was made to be in the Dark Kingdom." She smiled weakly.

Macho shook his head with a determined expression. "No. I want it to be you. That's all there is to it."

A tear rolled down Dust's face, then she turned away.

141

The Princess said, "So it's settled. I will have some of the flutter-fly ponies fly you back to the Jagged Line. A bunch of them are staying at the castle. It seems they recently figured out how to fly. You've made quite an impression, Macho. But anyway, shall I have them fly you both back?"

Dust and Macho briefly looked at each other then at the Princess. They nodded.

"Okay. Good luck." She picked up the bottle and started blowing bubbles again.

A few of them popped against Macho, but he was not in a bubbly mood.

Back to Pastel

142

The flutter-fly ponies flew Dust and Macho back to the Jagged Line using ropes attached to harnesses. Three flying ponies lifted Dust—three others lifted Macho. One flying poni carried Macho's ball. Superfly was one of the ponies, but chose not to speak a word, which was fine with Macho.

They got to the Jagged Line quickly and without incident. Flying was much faster than walking.

The flying ponies set Dust, Macho and the blue ball down in front of the Jagged Line, then flew off, because their obligation was done with. As they left, Superfly shouted, "Mofo!"

After Dust and Macho got out of their harnesses, they stared at each other in silence, not knowing what to say. They each wore one half of the amulet. Now it was time to bring them together.

Finally, Macho spoke. "Dust, I want you to know I don't regret this. I'm just glad to know that you'll be able to go back. I want you to go on with

your life and be happy."

They were both crying.

Dust said, "I'm so grateful. You've always been so kind to me. I never deserved someone like you."

"Of course you do, Dust. I saw all those things that nobody else saw. All the good things. They're the reason I fell in love with you. Ever since we were kids. I will always love you."

Dust nodded while the tears rolled from her eyes. "I know you will. Thank you so much for loving me. I don't think anyone else ever really did."

143

They nuzzled for a few moments, then Dust looked deeply into Macho's eyes. "Macho?" she said.

"Yes?"

"I'm sorry I laughed at you that time that you fell. If I could go back now, I would have helped you up."

"I know," Macho replied softly. And now it was time. "Take the amulet," he said.

Dust lifted the amulet off of his neck, then Macho helped her slip it over her neck.

The two halves had to be pressed together, then they would meld and the wearer's broken heart would be healed. That's what the Princess had said.

Macho tilted his head, then leaned forward— with his mouth, he pressed the two halves of the amulet together. He felt them slide together perfectly.

He pulled his head back.

He watched the two parts of the broken heart swing back apart.

All he could utter was, "What?"

Then Dust was saying, "Macho, Macho. Listen to me..."

Macho shook his head in disbelief. "It can't be. I must have done it wrong."

Dust was trying to comfort him, saying, "You didn't do it wrong."

Macho looked into her eyes, then said, "You...you didn't die of a broken heart. You never loved me."

"You were always too good for me. I should have loved you. I tried."

"But...you didn't."

"Maybe I just don't know how. It's not your fault."

"I was always too sweet for you...."

"Yes," Dust said, "but it's my fault. Don't you see? I'm broken. I belong here in the Dark Kingdom. *You* belong in the Pastel Kingdom."

"So tell me, if you didn't die of a broken heart, how *did* you die?"

"I chewed the petals of a poisonous flower called the lotus."

"Suicide? Why?"

"It was part of the deal. And Darkeyes was here. I wanted to be with him."

"Because he's dangerous," Macho said.

"Yes."

Machoponi

"Did you set me up on the night of the promenade?"

Dust looked down with shame. "Yes. Me and Badunkadunk...Clint told us to eat a bunch of mints, then kiss you so you would get intoxicated and lose the dance off. I'm so sorry."

"Why did you do it?"

"I don't know why, okay? Clint wanted to embarrass you. He told me to do it, so I did. He has a power over me."

Macho looked down at the ground, trying to hide the hurt in his eyes. "I still love you, Dust. I see the things in you that nobody else sees, not Clint or Darkeyes. I want you to know that. Let me stay with you. Here in the Dark Kingdom."

"No, Macho, you can't. The Dark Kingdom transforms all the undead. The undead don't know love. Besides, you belong on the pastel side. Please, if you love me like you say you do, go back for me."

Despite the pain, Macho replied, "Okay."

Macho transferred the two halves of the amulet to his neck.

Dust leaned forward and connected the two halves together with her mouth.

The two halves held together and started to glow with a white light. Macho felt the warmth on his skin.

He looked over at the gray girlponi in front of him. He wondered where she had come from.

The girlponi smiled at him, then said, "It worked. Now hurry, and cross over."

Macho kicked his ball across, then stepped across the Jagged Line. He was now back in his home: the Pastel Kingdom.

146

He turned to look back at the undead girlponi. "Thank you."

The undead poni had tears streaming from her eyes. "You're welcome, Macho."

"I'm sorry. Have we met?"

The undead girlponi looked taken aback. "What do you mean? Of course we have. It's me, Dust."

Macho smiled awkwardly. "I'm sorry. I don't recall. I'm so embarrassed. Perhaps if you refresh my memory..."

Sadness came over the undead girlponi's face. "It's no big deal. I'm just a girl. A girl you were always too good for."

Macho felt confused. "I'm sorry. I don't understand."

"Goodbye, Macho. I wish I could have been what you thought I was."

"Goodbye," Macho replied.

The girlponi turned and started walking away.

Macho watched her for a few moments, then he turned and started walking back to his village.

He squinted his eyes, because the Pastel Kingdom seemed so bright after having been in the Dark Kingdom.

The Legend of Machoponi
Part the Second

147

And so, our Hero crossed the line,
But could not say, "Fair Dust is mine."
The wind lifts feelings from his heart,
And Dust and Macho drift apart.

Sometimes, a brain freeze doesn't kill,
And cannot stop the tears that spill.
Sometimes, there's damage to the brain—
Lobotomy, along with pain.

And so, brain freeze lobotomy,
Offends like a smiling enemy.
The betrayer's acts, they bring such pain,
But roofies swipe it from the brain.

Forgotten flavors tease his soul,
Like gazing at an empty bowl.
And ice cream tasted yesterday,
Evaporates, to his dismay.
Dust drifts away.

ABOUT THE AUTHOR

Lotus, or Lotey, as he keeps trying to get people to call him, lives in Austin, an oasis in the heart of Texas. He attended the University of Texas at Austin, where he learned that frat boys are lame. He once watched a fraternity house burn down when they accidentally set their fake snow on fire after a party. After college, rather than get a real job, he decided to become a writer. He invented the corruptagram, a symbol he's trying to get banned in public schools. He enjoys Newcastle Brown Ale and black metal with blastbeats. Lotus Rose is not a frat boy.

myspace.com/lotus_rose
myspace.com/machoponi

Here's a short poem he wrote:

O, shall I be like the lotus,
And bring you dark dreams and soft sighs?
Or shall I be like the rose is,
Sweet-scented and tempting your eyes?

For the unending sleep can seduce you,
To the world behind unseeing eyes.
And the beauty that beckons, then cuts you,
Is also the cruelest of lies.

ABOUT THE ARTIST

Emma, or Emz as her friends like to call her, is a viking who lives in the most southern part of Sweden (no, there are no polar bears there). She is currently attending the University of Lund where she's trying to become an animal ecologist, only so she can torture animals in the name of science. In her free time she pretends to be an artist and likes to doodle on everything she can lay her hands on, including furniture, wallpaper and other people. She enjoys Monty Python, Simpsons, liquorice and kittens with dewdrops in their whiskers.

http://Honeykitten.deviantart.com

Favourite quote:
"Fantasy is hardly an escape from reality. It's a way of understanding it."
~ Lloyd Alexander

CPSIA information can be obtained at www.ICGtesting.com
Printed in the USA
BVOW020754121212

307979BV00004B/482/P

9 781933 929798